CHAO SHU-LI

CHANGES IN LI VILLAGE

Fredonia Books
Amsterdam, The Netherlands

Changes in Li Village

by
Chao Shu-li (Zhao Shuli)

ISBN: 1-4101-0813-9

Reprinted from the 1953 edition

Fredonia Books
Amsterdam, The Netherlands
http://www.fredoniabooks.com

CHARACTERS

OLD SUNG *village policeman and temple custodian*
LANDLORD LI *village head*
CHUN-HSI *Li's nephew, the village schoolmaster*
OLD WANG *manager of the grocery*
LITTLE MAO *Li's lackey*
TIEH-SO *a middle peasant*
ERH-NIU *Tieh-so's wife*
HSIAO-HSI *Li's nephew*
OLD CHEN *Erh-niu's grandfather*
OLD YANG *an old villager*
LENG-YUAN *a hot-headed youngster*
PAI-KOU *Erh-niu's younger brother*
LITTLE FATTY *Tieh-so's son*
WANG *a bandit*
DUCK NECK
THIN LIPS
DEEP-SET EYES *a group of petty officials looking for*
RAMROD *remunerative posts*
FATTY WEI
LITTLE CHANG *young Communist organizer*
CHIAO-CHIAO *Old Yang's daughter, Pai-kou's wife*
COMRADE WANG *a young cadre*

In Li Village there was a Dragon King Temple, and the man who looked after the temple was called Old Sung. Old Sung had a personal name too, but because he was so old nobody used it. And because his status was so low all the villagers, whether white-bearded old men or children who had just learned to talk, addressed him simply as Old Sung.

Eight or nine years before the War of Resistance to Japanese Aggression, Dragon King Temple was used both for village sacrifice and as the village administration office. Landlord Li was both village head and master of sacrifice; hence Old Sung also had two functions, serving concurrently as village policeman and temple custodian.

There was a bell hanging in the temple, the sound of which Old Sung loved to hear. This bell might be rung for two different reasons: if it only sounded three times (and it was always Old Sung who rang it in such cases), it meant sacrifice was in progress, while if rung at random it meant someone had a case to bring to court. When there was a sacrifice Old Sung could eat part of the offerings to the spirits, and when there was a case for the village administration he could eat one portion of the pancakes.

One day as Old Sung was having breakfast he heard the temple gate bang, and immediately after the bell sounded. Looking through the bamboo curtain, he saw that it was Chun-hsi, the village schoolmaster, who was ringing the bell.

Chun-hsi was a native of the village, and a nephew of Landlord Li. A few years earlier Old Sung would have called him Chun-hsi, but he was now considerably over twenty, had graduated from middle school and was teaching in the village school, so it would never do to call him Chun-hsi now. On the other hand, an old man of nearly sixty does not care to address a young fellow whom he has watched growing up as Mister. When Old Sung saw that it was he, although at a loss to know what to call him, he hurried out. When Chun-hsi had finished ringing the bell, the old man greeted him: "Come in and sit down! Who are you bringing a case against?"

Ignoring his greeting, Chun-hsi stepped inside and ordered him: "Go and report to the village head that Tieh-so has cut down my mulberry tree, and see when he can take up the case."

Old Sung did as he was told. In a short time he was back, and said: "The village head is not up yet. He says he will call a meeting at noon today."

"All right," said Chun-hsi. Then he stood up and walked out, without a glance behind.

Old Sung prepared his meal and put it in a big bowl (a bowl large enough to contain a whole meal), and with this in his hand he left the temple, locking the gate behind him. He had to notify all those whose attendance would be required at court, together with the plaintiff and defendant. He ate as he went, and by the time his meal was finished he had found everybody he wanted. Last of all he called at the general grocery, notified the manager Old Wang and bought twenty catties of white flour to take back to the temple. This flour was for making pancakes for the meeting. In the past, before there was any village administration office, the villagers would take any disputes they had to the masters of sacrifice to settle. And while the case was being heard a catty of pancakes per head was provided for the masters of sacrifice, the parties concerned, witnesses, temple custodian and other assistants. When the case was finished the successful party paid forty per cent of the expenditure while the loser paid sixty per cent. After the 1911 Revolution a village administration office had been set up. And later, when the Shansi warlord Yen Hsi-shan reorganized the villagers, an Arbitration Board was set up. But no matter what changes were made in Li Village, the old order swallowed up the new; thus when settling cases in the office they simply increased the portions of pancakes—in addition to the masters of sacrifice, parties concerned, witnesses and assistants, a portion each was added for the village head, deputy head, village elders and arbiters.

By midday, when the food was ready and everybody had arrived, a master of sacrifice called Little Mao opened the proceedings by distributing the pancakes. Landlord Li was both village head and a master of sacrifice, while Chun-hsi was both teacher and interested party; so they received double portions. All the others who held two positions also received double portions, according to custom, while those who held only one position received one portion. There were exceptions, however. For instance, Old Sung, although he was both village policeman and temple custodian, only received one portion. Although Little Mao himself had one portion, after the village head had eaten one bowl fried with eggs, as he invariably did, Little Mao could take home any that were left. And extra pancakes were usually prepared, in case anyone should turn up who was entitled to a portion.

After the pancakes had been eaten and the tables put together, the village head took his seat at the top. Old Wang, manager of the grocery shop, sat next to the village head, and the rest took their respective places.

"Let's start!" said Little Mao. "Sir! You are the plaintiff, you speak first."

"Very well," said Chun-hsi, "I'll speak first." With these words he pulled forward his chair, turned up his cuffs and sat up straight.

"I have a tumbledown latrine outside Tieh-so's south wall—"

"*You* have?" interrupted Tieh-so.

4

"What's this!" exclaimed Li. "No sense of what is fitting! It's not your turn to speak." Then, nodding to Chun-hsi, he said, "Proceed!"

"Close by the latrine was a small mulberry tree," Chun-hsi continued. "But not one single year have I been able to gather its leaves: as soon as they came out other people would pick them. Yesterday, toward evening, when my wife went to this tree to pick some leaves, Tieh-so's wife accused her of stealing their mulberry leaves. She seized hold of my wife and wouldn't let her go! Luckily I came across them on my way back from school, and remonstrated with her, and finally she released my wife. At first I meant to find Tieh-so, to tell him to keep his wife in order; but I didn't want to make a mountain out of a mole-hill, so I decided not to make an issue of it, and didn't go. But this morning when I went out I saw the mulberry tree had vanished, so I went straight to see Tieh-so. 'Tieh-so!' I said, as I walked into his house, 'who cut down that little mulberry tree next to the latrine?' 'I did!' said his wife. 'Why did you cut down my tree?' I asked. 'Yours?' she said. 'You'd better go and find out whose it was!' I wondered why I should have to ask other people about my own property, so I sounded the bell, and have come to ask you all to question him. That's all I have to say, let him speak! Let's see what excuse he has for cutting down the tree."

Li nodded toward Tieh-so. "Tieh-so! Speak up! Why did you cut down someone else's tree?"

"Why do you say it was his tree too?" asked Tieh-so.

"Before I've started questioning you, do you want to question me?" demanded Li. "You people from outside really have no sense of what is proper. Your family has been here for several generations and still not civilized!"

Little Mao also rebuked Tieh-so, saying, "Just give your reason. Why should you start contradicting the village head?"

"All right, all right," said Tieh-so, "I'll give my reason. I didn't plant that mulberry tree, it grew itself; but since it grew by my latrine wall, I suppose it was mine, wasn't it? But not one single year was I able to gather its leaves; the tree was always stripped bare by other people in less than no time...."

"Cut out the frills!" ordered Li. "Don't drag it out like that!"

"He dragged his out," said Tieh-so.

"There you go again!" said Little Mao. "Did you come to state your case, or to contradict the village head?"

"Why won't you let me speak?" asked Tieh-so.

"Never mind, never mind!" said Old Wang. "Quarrelling won't settle anything. As I see it, the dispute between the two parties centres in the actual ownership of the latrine. I suggest, Chun-hsi, since you say it is yours, you provide proof."

"It has been in our family for generations, what other proof do you want?" said Chun-hsi.

"And you, Tieh-so?" said Old Wang. "What proof do you have?"

"That court, the latrine included, was sold by his grandfather to my grandfather," said Tieh-so. "I have the deed." With these words he produced the deed from his pocket and handed it to Old Wang.

While the others crowded round to look at the deed, Li simply looked at Chun-hsi.

"Look well, all of you," said Chun-hsi. "Is it one latrine on his deed or two!"

"Of course it's one," said Tieh-so. "The one I'm using now, everybody knows, is one my father built later."

"Just putting a bold face on it won't do," said Li. "Do you remember it or not?"

"That was thirty years ago," said Tieh-so. "I'm only in my twenties, of course I don't remember it. But there are plenty of old people in the village. Let's call a few in and ask them!"

"You can argue," said Li. "Do you have to ask others? I'm over fifty myself, but I don't remember it."

"And I'm over forty," said Little Mao. "As I recall it there were two latrines there."

"Little Mao," said Tieh-so, "let's be honest!"

Li glared at Tieh-so and said, "According to you, everybody is conspiring to trick you, is that it?"

Realizing Li was about to lose his temper, Tieh-so took fright and muttered: "Well, I wouldn't care to say that!"

A woman outside the window suddenly called out: "Why wouldn't you? They *are* conspiring to trick you!" Thereupon Tieh-so's wife Erh-niu rushed in, holding a baby in one arm and gesticulating with the other, shouting: "Those over fifty don't remember! Those over forty remember there were two latrines!

Aren't there any other old folk in the village, or are you the only two left?"

Li banged the table. "Get out!" he exclaimed. "Lawless, shameless creature! Get out of here! Old Sung! Throw her out!"

"Throw me out?" said Erh-niu. "It was I who caught the thief, I who cut down the tree. Why won't you let me speak?"

"Did we send for you?" demanded Li.

"You ought to have," retorted Erh-niu. "How can you settle a case without calling the parties actually involved?"

"A family may have a thousand members, but only one head," said Little Mao. "Since your man is here, what is the use of calling you? Go on now, get out!"

"That won't do," said Erh-niu, throwing off his hand. "It's not a question of deciding who is stronger! I caught the thief! I cut down the tree! If I've done wrong, I'll take the blame. Don't drag my husband into it!"

More and more people were crowding round outside the window, nodding silently, some of them saying softly to their neighbours: "Erh-niu is right!"

While this argument was going on, a man came in through the temple gate. He was in his twenties. He had lank locks of hair, and was wearing a black silk jacket and carrying a cane walking stick. As if they had seen a snake in the path, the villagers gave a gasp of dismay and made way for him. This was Hsiao-hsi, another of Li's nephews, who had graduated from middle school, then started smoking opium, making friends with the rogues in the neighbourhood, selling young girls and widows, distributing opium, acting as a crooked lawyer.... He was capable of anything. He was now working for Third Master, the younger brother of Yen Hsi-shan's secretary, and this backing had made him more of a bully than ever. Everyone was afraid of him. As he entered he came directly upon Erh-niu. "What are you nattering about?" he demanded.

With the exception of the village head, who was his uncle, everyone else stood up smiling to greet Hsiao-hsi. But Erh-niu was not going to put up with abuse. "Is it any business of yours?" she retorted. "What is your place in the court? Who invited you?..."

Before she could finish, Hsiao-hsi slashed at her with his stick, exclaiming: "Get out of here at once! Law-breaker! Scum!"

"Sir!" put in Little Mao. "Don't pay any attention to her!" Then to Erh-niu: "Aren't you going yet?"

Erh-niu neither cried nor turned tail. Drawing herself up she defied Hsiao-hsi: "Come and kill me!"

Hsiao-hsi whirled his stick and brought it down heavily on her back twice, saying, "And what if I do kill you?" He hurt the baby's shoulder, so the child started howling.

When the people outside the window saw the ugly turn things were taking, they hurried in to drag Erh-niu away. Erh-niu, however, did not weaken, and turned her head to say: "So you are the only ones who can live! Outsiders don't stand a chance."

Some people urged her in a whisper:

"Don't say any more! Is this a time for talking about right and wrong? Do you suppose you can get the better of him?"

Inside, the village head issued an order: "Those with no business here go out! Why are you making such a disturbance outside?"

Little Mao pushed aside the screen and called out: "Haven't you seen the tiger head sign on the temple gate? 'Village Court. Only officers admitted.' What is all this disturbance? Get out now!"

So the watchers by the window had to go away, taking Erh-niu with them.

When Little Mao saw they had gone, he immediately turned back to attend to Hsiao-hsi: "Have a rest! Old Sung! Are the pancakes still warm?"

Old Sung brought over a dish of pancakes, saying: "They were by the fire! They're not too cold yet!" As he spoke he placed them respectfully before Hsiao-hsi.

Hsiao-hsi showed no false modesty but fell to on the pancakes, and as he ate he said, "I've just got back from Third Master's place. Third Master asked me to buy him a good tea-stand, I wonder if there is one in the village."

"Presently we will make enquiries!" said Little Mao. "There may be!"

"Is everyone very busy at Third Master's?" asked Li.

"Yes," said Hsiao-hsi, with his mouth full of pancake. And nodding his head, he went on: "There is too much to do! Third Master doesn't want to attend to all those things, but everyone insists on it!

Nearly all the matters that the county government can't settle are referred to him!" Old Sung served him a bowl of soup. Hsiao-hsi took two sips, then catching sight of Tieh-so he put down the bowl and said: "Tieh-so, you need to teach that wife of yours a good lesson! Look at the way she behaves! Letting her tongue run away with her without any sense of shame! Do you want her to become a laughing stock?"

"He beats my wife and now he wants to lecture me," thought Tieh-so. "What is the world coming to?" But circumstances were against him. It was no use appealing to justice, so he had to hold his tongue.

After a while Hsiao-hsi's soup was nearly finished, but less than a third of the pancakes had been eaten. Old Wang proposed: "Let's get on with the business!"

"I don't know what this is about," said Hsiao-hsi, standing up. "I've still got to buy a tea-stand for Third Master."

"Have some more to eat before you go," said Little Mao.

Hsiao-hsi rolled up all the pancakes in the dish, and picked them up saying, "Right! I'll take these along!" Then, the pancakes in one hand and his walking stick in the other, he left hurriedly.

Old Wang continued: "Tieh-so! You say the latrine you are using now was built by your father. Can you bring witnesses to confirm that?"

"Certainly I can," said Tieh-so. "Do you imagine my neighbour Old Chen will have forgotten?"

"He won't do!" said Chun-hsi. "In the first place he's from the same county as you, and in the second place he's your wife's grandfather, so of course he'll say anything you want."

"Well then, we won't ask him," said Tieh-so. "What about Old Yang? He's a native here anyway."

"He won't do either!" said Chun-hsi. "Your brother-in-law Pai-kou is going to marry Old Yang's daughter, so that connects him with your family too."

"You'll find it hard to object to everyone," said Tieh-so. "There are so many old people in the village!" He pointed at Old Sung. "Old Sung is between fifty and sixty, and he's not connected with me in any way, is he?"

"Old Sung is a poor temple custodian," protested Little Mao. "What does he know about anything? You just ask him whether he dares to act as witness or not. Old Sung! Do you remember this or not?"

Naturally Old Sung remembered, but if he were to tell the truth that would be the end of his living in the temple, so he evaded the issue. "I've always been poor," he said, "thinking all the time how to fill my stomach, never paying attention to anything else."

"Since there is a deed, let's go by that," said Li. "On the deed there is only one, so how can you demand two from him? And what's the point of looking for witnesses? Although there are so many old people in the village, it's not their business to protect your property."

"What about this," said Little Mao, "I think we had better adjourn the meeting to talk it over. We are not getting anywhere like this."

Everybody agreed, and some of them gathered in groups to exchange views. Little Mao, the village head and Chun-hsi made signs with their fingers for some time, while Old Wang discussed the real crux of the matter with the village elders. Then Little Mao went over to Old Wang and said: "What about this! Their idea is to have Tieh-so pay so much!" As he spoke he took Wang's hand to convey the amount, asking, "What do you think?"

Wang answered in a low voice, "To tell the truth, it is this latrine that was sold by Chun-hsi's grandfather as stated in the deed. That one Tieh-so is using really was built by his father Carpenter Chang. I think you ought to remember this."

"It's not a question of remembering or not," replied Little Mao. "If we stick to the truth we shall offend too many people. Just think, the village head and Chun-hsi both want him to pay damages. And then there's Hsiao-hsi—Tieh-so can't afford to offend them, and neither can I!"

Wang said nothing, simply shaking his head. The village elders dared not make any proposals, all watching Wang, the village head and Little Mao. Evening began to fall, yet still they had come to no decision, so all went home to eat.

That evening Old Sung went from house to house again to summon them back. Old Wang said he was unwell and could not attend. Of the rest, some went and some did not. In the temple they kept silent, and the village head passed sentence: The latrine was Chun-hsi's, Tieh-so should pay two hundred dollars for the mulberry tree he had cut down, and also all the cost of pancakes and expenses of the meeting. And he was ordered to produce a guarantor before leaving the temple.

2

OLD CHEN ACTED AS GUARANTOR. HE GUARANTEED that the money would be paid within a month, and only then was Tieh-so allowed to leave the temple. Tieh-so could scarcely hold up his head for rage, and Old Chen took his arm to help him home. As soon as he reached home he threw himself on the bed and burst into tears. When Erh-niu questioned him he could not answer, and Old Chen could not get him to stop crying. Presently all the neighbours had heard and hurried over to ask what had happened, but Tieh-so was still crying too much to speak, and it was Old Chen who told them the verdict of the village administration office point by point, saying: "It was decided the latrine was Chun-hsi's, and Tieh-so was ordered to pay him two hundred dollars, and to bear all expenses of the meeting."

Hearing Old Chen reopen the subject, Tieh-so sobbed even more bitterly. All the neighbours shook their heads, and Erh-niu said, "It's all very fine for them to talk!" She put the baby down in front of Tieh-so, saying: "I'm giving you the baby! You leave this business to me! We won't pay him, and we won't let him take the latrine! I started this business! It's between him and me! I don't care what happens to me! Anyway we can't leave it at this!" She jumped down from the bed and started to rush outside, and it took seven or eight of the neighbours to restrain her. The baby on the bed started howling at the top of its voice, and Old Chen hastily picked it up.

The others reasoned with them separately and succeeded in calming Erh-niu for the time being, while Tieh-so stopped crying. "This is going too far!" said Old Yang to Old Chen. "Not only you people from outside, but even we natives have an impossible time of it. Look how many cases crop up in the village each year, and every single case is engineered by them. And nothing we can do about it!"

A youngster in the group, called Leng-yuan, jumped up and said: "Tieh-so! Why don't you go and wait for him by the road at the top of the cliff? If you had any guts you would knock him down with your hoe!"

"You young people really have no sense," said Old Yang. "When he's in such a rage how can you talk so wildly to him?"

This checked Leng-yuan, and the other youngsters pointed at him and jeered: "Cold feet! Cold feet!"[1]

---

[1] In Chinese this is a pun. "Leng" means cold.

After a short silence Old Chen said, "I think you should report this to the higher authorities. Even if you lose your case in the county seat it will be better for you than this."

"That's a possibility," said Old Yang. "In the county court at least they can't just hear one side. They will have to question witnesses."

"This business is really the limit!" said Leng-yuan. "What a pity I am too young to remember, otherwise I would ask you to accept me as a witness!"

"You may be too young," said Yang. "But others are older!"

Several people over thirty exclaimed together: "It isn't so long since Tieh-so's father built that latrine. Practically everyone over thirty must remember."

"In your complaint put down anyone you like. We are all willing to bear witness."

"Put down a good few. Doesn't matter if we all go!"

"Let's go to the county court then," said Erh-niu, "and have it out with him. Even if we spend our last cent we can't let them get away with this!" Then she said to Old Chen: "Grandfather, you are always saying how our family came here practically empty-handed; now even if the worst happens we will only be going away empty-handed again, and at least we managed to grow up here. So what is there to worry about!"

While they were speaking, Erh-niu's teen-age brother Pai-kou ran in saying, "Sister! Mother's here!"

As Erh-niu got up to go and meet her, her mother came in and said in a low voice: "What are you all discussing?"

"Discussing complaining to the authorities!" shouted Leng-yuan.

Erh-niu's mother signed to him to be quiet, and said: "That Chun-hsi's wife is listening outside the window."

"Let her listen!" said Erh-niu. "Can she stop me taking the case to court?"

The news that someone was eavesdropping resulted in a general silence. "See if you can't make her see reason!" the neighbours said to Erh-niu's mother, and then slowly took their leave.

The return of Li and his nephews was quite a different story. Chun-hsi, Hsiao-hsi and Little Mao gathered in Li's big courtyard and closed the big black gate to celebrate their victory. Having eaten pancakes in the afternoon they were not hungry, so Chun-hsi did not prepare another meal but just bought ten dollars' worth of opium (fifty sticks) to express his thanks. When Li had smoked his fill Little Mao might take a few puffs after him, but no one else was allowed to use his Taiku opium lamp or Yihsing pottery pipe, accordingly Chun-hsi had brought his own smoking equipment with him. Li had an inner and an outer room. By the opium lamp in the inner room Little Mao prepared Li's pipe for him, while the two cousins lay down by the lamp in the outer room. The inner room was quiet because Li considered Little Mao fit only to prepare his pipe, and Little Mao, standing in awe of Li, did not dare appear too forward. Little Mao fitted a stick of opium to the pipe, and Li smoked it; and after he had smoked seven or eight in a row, Little Mao cleared the ash out of the pipe and filled it up again. When this process had been repeated, Li smoked the accumulated ash, and went to sleep. But by the time Little Mao had prepared another pipe, fitted the stick to the pipe and put it to his own mouth, Li suddenly woke up and started smoking again.

Although there were only Hsiao-hsi and Chun-hsi in the outer room, they were much more lively. They had many topics of conversation. First they spoke of Third Master's wealth and power, then about various pretty girls and passable wives they knew, and finally of their victory that day. When Erh-niu's name came up, Chun-hsi said: "You really laid into her properly! I was just at a loss how to deal with her, but as soon as you came in the matter was settled."

"The medicine varies according to the sickness," said Hsiao-hsi. "If we couldn't even get the better of a common woman how could we ever get on in future? You're really no good, Cousin! As I see it, you will have to be content to be a teacher all your life."

"Although she is only a common woman," retorted Chun-hsi, "still she's very capable! She has all her wits about her!"

"Bah ...." Hsiao-hsi shook his head. "I was wondering why you couldn't deal with her, but you seem to have taken a fancy to her." As he spoke he pointed his opium pin at his cousin's nose. "If your wife knew, you'd have to kneel to her half the night!

Good-for-nothing! Greenhorn! Fancy getting interested in such an ordinary woman!"

Chun-hsi wanted to protest vehemently, but could not find a suitable retort. Hsiao-hsi threw his head back on the pillow and burst out laughing, and Chunhsi had to join in his laughter. Just then Li called out from inside: "Keep quiet! Listen, who's that knocking at the gate?" They both stopped laughing, and sure enough they could hear the door-knocker banging.

Little Mao ran out into the courtyard and asked, "Who's there?"

A woman's voice answered, "It's me! Open the door!"

Hsiao-hsi recognized Chun-hsi's wife's voice, and said with a laugh: "So your wife really has come to find you!"

Little Mao opened the door, and Chun-hsi's wife came in. "What's the matter?" asked Chun-hsi.

His wife answered quietly, "You go and listen to what that Erh-niu is saying in her home." At the mention of Erh-niu, Hsiao-hsi pointed at Chun-hsi again and burst out laughing, and Chun-hsi laughed too. His wife could not make head or tail of it, and asked hastily, "What's the matter?"

"That's a secret," said Hsiao-hsi. "You mustn't ask. Tell us what you heard Erh-niu say."

Chun-hsi's wife sat down behind Hsiao-hsi, leaning against him and facing Chun-hsi, and described in detail Leng-yuan's reckless proposal, and how Erh-niu was willing to spend the whole family fortune on bringing the case to the county court.

Before Chun-hsi could reply, Hsiao-hsi gave her a shove, and said, "Go back now, go on! It doesn't matter! Who can she hurt even if she does take it to the county court? And if he lies in wait at the top of the cliff we'll see who is the braver!" Chun-hsi also told his wife to go home, so she left. Little Mao closed the gate again, and Hsiao-hsi went on bragging.

From the inner room Li called out softly and sleepily: "Hsiao-hsi!... Come here!..." And Hsiao-hsi went in. As soon as Little Mao saw him he got up and offered him his place on the bed, sitting down himself on a stool by the bed to listen. Li looked at Little Mao, then picked up three or four sticks of opium and gave them to him, saying, "You go and lie down outside." Seeing that they did not want him to listen, Little Mao had to take the opium to the outer room to smoke.

Little Mao had just finished the first stick and was burning the ash when Hsiao-hsi came out. And then, of course, he had to get up again to offer him the place on the bed. "Cousin," said Hsiao-hsi to Chun-hsi, "Uncle says if that creature really intends to take the case to court, you'll have to do something about it."

"Well, then we'll have to think of some way out," put in Little Mao from the side.

When Hsiao-hsi realized Little Mao was still there, he regretted having shown signs of weakness, and, immediately getting on his high horse again, said, "Of course there is a way out!"

"How ridiculous!" said Chun-hsi. "A country clod like that, what could he get out of appealing to the county court?"

Hsiao-hsi looked at Little Mao and said, "You go back inside again!" When Little Mao had picked up his opium and gone back in again, Hsiao-hsi said in a low voice: "Of course we're not afraid of losing the case in court! But Uncle says we mustn't let him take such a step. No matter whether he was found to be in the right or not, once it was said a country bumpkin had brought a case against us, we should lose a lot of face."

"Well, but how can we stop him?" asked Chun-hsi.

"That riffraff!" said Hsiao-hsi. "Why should you treat them so politely? Just think of some way so that he can't go to court!"

"Think of what way?"

"Don't be afraid," said his cousin. "There's Third Master. Tomorrow morning, first thing, I'll go to see him."

That evening they smoked till very late before going home.

The next morning Hsiao-hsi went to see Third Master, while Tieh-so made haste to borrow money in order to take his case to court. But since it was the fourth month of the lunar calendar, the country people were all busy; and none of them had cash in hand anyway. Tieh-so spent the whole morning hurrying from house to house, borrowing a dollar from one and fifty cents from another. With great difficulty he succeeded in raising four or five dollars. Erh-niu too was busy at home grinding flour and making rolls for Tieh-so to take to town as provisions.

That afternoon, just as Tieh-so and Erh-niu were having their meal, Hsiao-hsi came in with another man, carrying a rope, who snatched away Tieh-so's bowl and tied him up.

"What are you doing?" exclaimed Erh-niu. "What is his crime this time?"

"No need to ask!" said Hsiao-hsi. "You're in it too!" So saying he seized Erh-niu's baby and threw it on the ground, then tied her up too. Some villagers were sitting at the crossroads eating, and when they saw Hsiao-hsi and a stranger with a rope going to Tieh-so's house they knew there was trouble brewing. Old Yang, Old Chen and Leng-yuan, who were Tieh-so's neighbours, went to see what was the matter. They found Tieh-so and his wife tied up, and the baby crying on the ground. But before they could ask what the trouble was, Hsiao-hsi pointed his cane at Leng-yuan and said, "There's another of them! Tie him up, tie him up!" Then the stranger tied up Leng-yuan too.

The two men led their three prisoners out, followed by Old Chen, who had picked up the baby, and some other neighbours. The more timid people on the road were afraid of being involved themselves, and went away; but Erh-niu's father, mother and brothers, and Leng-yuan's father and mother caught up with them on the road and followed them. When they saw the fierce expression on the faces of Hsiao-hsi and the man he had brought with him, they dared not question them; only Old Chen and Leng-yuan's father drew abreast of Hsiao-hsi, pleading with him as they walked.

Hsiao-hsi took them to the temple, and said to Old Sung: "Go and ask the village head to come!" And Old Sung went as he was told.

"Hsiao-hsi!" appealed Old Chen. "We're all neighbours, and should be able to settle any trouble among ourselves. If young people talk foolishly, we must beg you to be broad-minded and make allowances."

"You know what happened as well as I do," said Hsiao-hsi. "These people plotted to wait at the edge of the cliff to assassinate the village head. The village head, learning of this, sent me to see Third Master; and as soon as I reported the matter to Third Master he said, 'These people are bandits. First have them tied up, and then we'll discuss it!' From all accounts there are others in it too. When they've been questioned, we shall be able to find out who their confederates are!"

When Erh-niu heard this she said, "When I caught that thief, I caught myself a lot of trouble: I've even become a bandit! Tell me, whom have I killed, whom have I robbed?"

"You brazen bandit!" said Hsiao-hsi. "Let's see how long you will go on brazening things out!"

"What a woman!" said Old Chen. "Can't you hold your tongue!"

When Li arrived with Little Mao at his heels, Hsiao-hsi told him: "Third Master told me to have them tied up and taken to him. You had better order some guards to take them into town straight away."

Old Chen saw that the position was desperate, so he gave the baby to his grandson Pai-kou, and taking hold of Little Mao said, "Let me have a word with you!" Then, drawing Little Mao outside the gate, he said, "I must ask you to talk this over with the village head and Hsiao-hsi, and see whether it can't be settled in the village."

Little Mao knew Hsiao-hsi fairly well: if he had money he would agree to anything. Moreover, if the case could be tried again in the village, no matter whatever the outcome he would be bound to make something out of it himself. At least he could eat some good things. So he answered most obligingly: "Certainly! I'll go and see what I can do for you! Of course I feel just like everybody else. I don't want any trouble in our village." Thereupon he hurried over to Hsiao-hsi and said, "Hsiao-hsi, come here! I've something to tell you!"

"What is it?"

Little Mao nodded as he repeated, "Come on, over here!" With a great show of reluctance Hsiao-hsi followed him into the Dragon King Hall.

Pai-kou was standing by Erh-niu, holding Little Fatty, and the child held out his two little hands to his mother. When Erh-niu moved to caress him, she realized her hands had been tied, and exclaimed with an angry glare: "Kill the child too! We might as well all die!" But although she spoke so defiantly, there were tears in her eyes. When her mother saw this she was very distressed, and cried herself as she wiped Erh-niu's tears.

Hsiao-hsi then emerged from the Dragon King Hall saying, "I don't see how it can be done! These wild people only cry when death is staring them in the face. We must take them over."

"Never mind," put in Little Mao from behind. "Let's talk it over calmly! There must be some way out of this, there's nothing that can't be settled peaceably! Village Head, let us go! Let's go with Hsiao-hsi to your house to talk this over."

Hsiao-hsi ordered his thug: "Watch them! If we can't reach an agreement we still have to take them to town!" So saying he went out first with the village head.

"You must first buy two lots of opium!" Little Mao whispered to Old Chen.

"I don't know where to buy it," said Old Chen.

"Just bring twenty dollars then," said Little Mao, "and I'll get it for you!"

Old Chen and Leng-yuan's father answered together: "All right! You buy it for us!" Then Little Mao went out after the village head and Hsiao-hsi.

Hsiao-hsi said that each person would have to pay one hundred and fifty dollars to Third Master, so the three of them would have to pay four hundred and fifty dollars altogether. One side fixed the price and the other side tried to bargain it down, while Little Mao acted both as witch doctor and devil, running from one party to the other. Only by evening was an agreement reached. The three of them together must pay one hundred and fifty dollars to Third Master. They must give Hsiao-hsi and the man he had brought with him fifty dollars for expenses. Tieh-so and Leng-yuan's families must give them a feast to acknowledge their fault, and they must sign a written statement guaranteeing the safety of the village head. The original sentence still stood, and must be carried out according to the verdict rendered by the village administration office the previous day.

Once the price had been fixed, Little Mao said they must pay in full. Old Chen went to the temple to discuss it with Tieh-so, and the latter, knowing there was nothing he could do about it, had to control his anger as best he could. At first Erh-niu was unwilling, but since she could think of no other way out she had to acquiesce. And Leng-yuan expressed no opinion, because since he had got into trouble on Tieh-so's account the latter would have to pay for him too. When Old Chen saw that they agreed, he went to look for Old Yang to act as guarantor with him, and the three young people were allowed out on bail.

This time when they were bailed out it was not like the previous day: Chun-hsi might be willing to be paid a month later, but Hsiao-hsi insisted on cash down. Tieh-so asked Old Chen and Old Yang to borrow the money from the grocery shop. However, Wang said he was just buying in raw silk and had no money to lend. Small sums, yes, but not more than a hundred dollars.

"Wang's shop is no good," said Old Yang. "And there is no other possibility in the village. We'll have to see Little Mao again and ask him to ask Hsiao-hsi to reconsider it, then we can borrow from Sixth Master."

"If Tieh-so borrows two hundred dollars from him, it will ruin him," said Old Chen.

"Well, there is nothing else for it," said Old Yang. "They will have to go through with it." Accordingly Old Chen went to speak to Tieh-so again.

This Sixth Master was an uncle of Third Master. He did not lend money like other people, but demanded thirty per cent interest each month; thus after three months he would recover his whole principal. Such a high rate of interest was fairly common in the old days, but the difference lay in his procedure of lending and getting the money back. People like Hsiao-hsi acted as his agents in lending money out, and were called guarantors. Usually, if a debtor could not pay up at the time specified, the terms of the contract allowed him to mortgage his property; but Sixth Master's contract stipulated: "When the period of loan has expired, if the principal has not been returned in full, the guarantor will act on behalf of the creditor and sell the property to repay the debt." In this way, although he had never confiscated anyone's property, neither had anyone ever failed to pay up. When Hsiao-hsi and his sort lent money, it was eighty instead of a hundred. That is, the contract said one hundred dollars but in actual fact only eighty were lent, the guarantor taking a rake-off of twenty dollars. "Eighty for a hundred, thirty per cent interest, three months' loan, at the end of that time the principal to be repaid in full, additional loans only granted on the same conditions, and in default of payment the property to be sold by the guarantor. ..." Such were the terms on which Sixth Master lent money. Under these circumstances, unless there was a dead man waiting to be buried, or someone was dying, no one dared borrow from him. But now Tieh-so was in a position where he had to borrow.

When Old Chen talked it over with Tieh-so, the latter could think of no other solution. He had to ask Little Mao to go and tell Hsiao-hsi to set down on the contract as security for Sixth Master's two hundred and fifty (which was actually only two hundred) two and a half acres of land which his grandfather and father had cultivated for two generations. Only so were they able to satisfy Third Master and Hsiao-hsi. Two lots of pancakes, a feast and the opium, cost thirty dollars, and this they borrowed from Old Wang.

On the third day, after the feast, the business could at last be considered settled.

Tieh-so owed Chun-hsi two hundred dollars, Sixth Master two hundred and fifty dollars, and Old Wang thirty dollars, making a total debt of four hundred and eighty dollars.

Hsiao-hsi made fifty dollars out of the system of eighty for a hundred, and received another fifty for expenses. He had hired the thug for two dollars, so that deducting these two dollars his actual gain was ninety-eight dollars.

And Landlord Li did not lose out either. Although Hsiao-hsi said Third Master must be paid one hundred and fifty dollars, they only gave him one hundred, the remaining fifty going to Li.

All Little Mao gained was two days of good food and ample opium.

A month later the silkworms were grown and wheat was ripe. The time had come for Tieh-so to pay the two hundred dollars due to Chun-hsi and the thirty dollars borrowed from Old Wang; and he was panic-stricken when he thought of the two hundred and fifty he owed Sixth Master. He decided "Better sell some property at once, rather than pay this terrible interest. If I wait another six months, even if all my property is sold it won't be enough for him." Having reached this decision, he gave Old Wang his raw silk and two bushels of wheat to clear the thirty dollars, sold one and a half acres of land to Li to pay off the two hundred and fifty dollars to Sixth Master, and made over his house to Chun-hsi with an additional three bushels of wheat to bring the value up to two hundred dollars. He himself moved into a stable on the roadside outside his old courtyard, this, and a single acre of land, being all that remained to him. Chun-hsi had many brothers and the house that had fallen to his share was a small one, so now that he had Tieh-so's property he was delighted. He hired workmen to repair the roof, patch the ceiling, whitewash the walls and revarnish the gate, until very soon the place was looking spick and span. The repairs done, he and his wife moved in. As for Tieh-so, he moved into the old stable where just the hoe and plough, pots and pans, plates, chopsticks and baskets took up two of the three rooms. The third room had a feeding trough in the middle, and in front of this trough he set up the stove, on top of the trough they made their bed. There was not even room for a water container.

In such a hovel, confronted every morning when he got up by the newly painted gate and gilded door-plate opposite, Tieh-so could not help feeling angry. Soon he fell ill, and lay sick for several months, the medicine he took proving no use. The proverb says, "A broken heart can only be cured by happiness." Later Third Master went to Taiyuan, accompanied by Hsiao-hsi and Chun-hsi. Some said that over a hundred families in the county had signed a charge against him and so the provincial government had them arrested. Others claimed that Third Master's elder brother, who was Yen Hsi-shan's secretary-general and a very high official, had heard how badly he was behaving and summoned him to the provincial capital to have him locked up. All agreed, at any rate, that Third Master was in trouble. When Tieh-so heard this his heart felt lighter, and his illness took a turn for the better.

3

After Tieh-so lost his property and fell ill, life became harder for them every day. Fortunately he had of his own free will learned carpentry and masonry from his father, and although he had never made a trade of it he was an able assistant. So now, shouldering his tools, he left the village and joined a group of workmen to earn a little extra cash.

In the summer of 1930 one of Yen Hsi-shan's subordinates, General Li, wanted to build a house in Taiyuan, and some of Tieh-so's former mates who had been hired for the job sent a man to tell him to join them. Tieh-so had heard that wages were high in Taiyuan; he also hoped to find out there what had really happened to Third Master; and Little Fatty had been weaned, so that Erh-niu was quite able to cultivate their acre of land. For these three reasons he agreed to go. In a few days he had prepared food for the road, travelling expenses, clothing, shoes and socks, and left with several others for Taiyuan.

However, this was the time when Yen Hsi-shan called his troops the Third People's Revolutionary Army, and in his fight with Chiang Kai-shek had almost reached Peking. Because of these victories, General Li decided he would build himself a house in Peking later, and sent a telegram to his steward in Taiyuan telling him to stop work there for the time being. Since work was called off, Tieh-so and the others had nothing to do, and had to find rooms in their county hostel in which to stay for the interim. No charge was made for rooms in the county hostel, but unfortunately they had not been there more than four or five days when a notice was posted on the door of their house: "Reserved for the Forty-eighth Division," and they were told they must find new quarters that same day. They had to rent rooms outside and move out.

Heavy rain a few days later reminded Tieh-so that he had left an old pair of shoes under the bed in the county hostel, so he went back to look for them. As soon as he went in, he saw that the room had changed completely: the floor was swept clean, table and chairs placed in good order, on the table was a big inkstone box some six inches long with a box for sealing ink and other elegant stationery. The bedding was spotless, and on the bed lay a man in a fine army uniform smoking opium. As soon as the man on the bed raised his head, Tieh-so saw that it was Hsiao-hsi. He felt as if he had come on a snake in his path, and started backing out, afraid there would be more trouble and not knowing the best thing to do. But Hsiao-hsi calmly and unhurriedly smiled at him, saying, "Tieh-so? Well, well! When did you get here? Come on in!"

This was the first time Tieh-so had ever been treated so politely by Hsiao-hsi. He did not know what the other's real intentions were, but it seemed he was in no immediate danger; moreover since they came from the same village, if Hsiao-hsi asked him in he could not well refuse. There was nothing for it but to go in and stand by the bed. Hsiao-hsi inclined his head towards the cigarettes beside the tray, saying, "Have a cigarette!" Tieh-so felt he was not the sort of person who ought to be treated to cigarettes, and he was about to decline politely when Hsiao-hsi picked up a cigarette and handed it to him, saying, "Go on!" Overwhelmed by the other's condescension, he accepted the cigarette very respectfully, lit it at the opium lamp, and stood by the side of the bed smoking. As he was smoking he puzzled over the reasan for Hsiao-hsi's politeness to him, but could not make it out. Although Hsiao-hsi still addressed him as a subordinate, he questioned him most amiably on all that had happened—asking him with whom he had come, what he was doing now, where he lived, whether he was being paid or not.... When he had ascertained that Tieh-so was out of work, he said, "Poor people like you can't afford to be idle. Since we come from the same village, now that you're in difficulties I ought to help you, only I don't know any family where they need workmen. But why don't you come here as my bodyguard?"

In view of Hsiao-hsi's concern, Tieh-so was willing to accept help from him; only because the other was in army uniform he was afraid he might have to become a soldier too. "Is a bodyguard the same as a soldier?" he asked.

"There are different kinds of soldiers," answered Hsiao-hsi, immediately understanding his scruples. "A bodyguard doesn't fight, and is not transferred from place to place. You would just stay here to keep the room in order, pour tea for guests, and run errands. As for the pay, it would be eight dollars a month, and each time guests came to play mahjong you would be able to make more in tips—isn't that the kind of job everybody wants? Several people have asked for the place, but I haven't accepted any of them yet. I'm only asking you because you are unemployed, and I want to help you; but of course don't take it if you don't want to."

While he was speaking they heard the sound of a bicycle in the courtyard and the tramp of leather shoes, and presently another man in uniform came in. Hsiao-hsi immediately got up and asked him to be seated, and Tieh-so retreated from the side of the bed to the window. The newcomer did not stand on ceremony, but went over to the bed and lay down opposite Hsiao-hsi. Hsiao-hsi pointed Tieh-so out to him and said, "Chief of staff, I am engaging a bodyguard for us! From my village. Very loyal! Very honest!"

"That's all right," the other answered off-handedly.

"Tieh-so, you go back and think it over," said Hsiao-hsi. "If you want to come, then come back this evening; and if you don't want to come, let me know so that I can get someone else!"

Although Tieh-so could not make up his mind whether to take the job or not, he felt it was high time for him to leave, so he replied promptly: "Right! Then I'll be going!"

Hsiao-hsi did not get up to see him out, just saying, "Very well." And he went out.

"That young fellow seems quite able," said the chief of staff, "but he doesn't strike me as bold enough. He's tongue-tied before strangers."

"Not necessarily," said Hsiao-hsi. "Only he dare not put on airs before me, because in the past I was over him."

"Whatever made you think of a bodyguard?" asked the chief of staff.

"I was just going to tell you," said Hsiao-hsi. As he was speaking he took out a packet of heroin and handed it to the chief of staff. He then helped himself to another cigarette, and while he was rolling a piece of paper round the cigarette (to smoke heroin) said: "Just now a waiter from Cheng Ta Hotel was searching the streets for the Forty-eighth Division Headquarters, saying that a visitor from Honan was looking for it. Finally the police station directed him here. I told him there was no responsible person here today, and asked the visitor to come tomorrow. I meant to have a smoke and then go to your house to report this, when that fellow from my village came in, and we had scarcely said more than a few words when you arrived."

Now Hsiao-hsi was only an adjutant with the rank of captain while the other was chief of staff. With such a discrepancy in rank, Hsiao-hsi ought to have reported all developments promptly, and his language ought to have been more respectful. Yet here he was lying at his ease beside his superior officer and talking in this casual manner. The reason was that the Forty-eighth Division was one that Yen Hsi-shan meant to set up, but as yet he had only appointed a division commander. The chief of staff had been recommended by the division commander, and to date there was not a single soldier, all future developments depending on the commander's skill. The commander's name was Huo, and he had previously had some dealings with the bandits in northern Honan Province—in fact he owed his position to this qualification. "As long as we have a name," he said, "there will be no difficulty about getting men!" Hsiao-hsi understood such things. The chief of staff was a graduate of the Imperial University in Japan, but every man has his limitations, and it was more difficult for him to establish contact with bandits than for Hsiao-hsi. Moreover Hsiao-hsi was connected with the secretary general, and the chief of staff had therefore to allow him certain liberties.

When Hsiao-hsi explained why he had not reported immediately, the other said nothing, so he offered him the heroin cigarette that he had finished rolling, and said: "I think this guest may be Old Huo (the division commander), who, having made his contacts, is now coming to establish contact with us. Since he is living at Cheng Ta Hotel (where only high officials stayed), he must be giving himself airs, and we ought to make this headquarters of ours a little more impressive if we don't want him to look down on us. This is the reason for my looking for a bodyguard."

The chief of staff listened to Hsiao-hsi's account approvingly, and commended him: "Right! This is absolutely necessary! I think in addition to a body-guard we should have some guards at the door. There are several men looking for work over at my place; when I go back I will send a couple over. This afternoon you can train them and issue each with one of those uniforms we were given." Having decided on this plan of action, the chief of staff stayed to smoke and chat for a while, and then went home.

Tieh-so was a puzzled man as he left the hostel. "What has come over Hsiao-hsi to make him so polite?" he wondered. "Why is he suddenly so good to me? Could it be a plot? But he seemed quite sincere, and I'm only a poor workman now, so what plot could he be brewing? Could he really want to help an old neighbour? Hsiao-hsi never does anything that is not to his own advantage." He came to the conclusion that there were two possibilities. Either Hsiao-hsi needed a servant and being unable for the moment to find anyone reliable, had asked him; or Hsiao-hsi felt compunction at having treated him badly in the past, and had decided to do him a good turn to make amends.

"If it's for the first reason," he reflected, "he needs a servant and I earn some money: that's a fair exchange. And although it means taking orders from him, beggars can't be choosers. If it's for the second reason, that is even better: the grudge I have against him can be worked off in this life, and there need be no vengeance in a future life." For Tieh-so still believed that a man has more lives than one, and avenges injuries in a later life.

"No matter whether it is for the first reason or the second," he decided, "either way I can't come to any harm. I might as well take it on." He really believed that Hsiao-hsi had changed for the better. On his return to his lodgings he told some of his mates, and although they thought someone like Hsiao-hsi could not change for the better in a thousand years, they approved his taking on the job, thinking the first reason which he suggested was right.

So the matter was settled. Tieh-so got together his things, and moved over to the hostel.

When Tieh-so reached the hostel the two men sent by the chief of staff had arrived, and Hsiao-hsi was giving them instructions in the courtyard as to how to stand, how to salute officials, how to challenge ordinary citizens, how to treat different kinds of guests, how to bring in visitors' cards. He also told Tieh-so how to fetch water, serve tea, light cigarettes and do other jobs. Hsiao-hsi was like a stage-manager, now taking the part of a guest, now of a servant. After making the three of them rehearse for a whole afternoon, he issued the uniforms and insignia, ready to receive the guest the next day.

The next morning the chief of staff came over before breakfast. He asked how the preparations were going and then had a meal in the hostel, after which he lay down as usual with Hsiao-hsi, smoking and discussing how to treat this unknown bandit chieftain. He heartily approved Hsiao-hsi's assertion that the right way to treat such people was with a mixture of politeness and haughtiness, courtesy and familiarity. When they had agreed on the plans, they chatted on various topics as they waited for the guards to bring in a visitor's card.

The two guards outside had never served in the army. Wearing new uniforms and carrying guns was such a novelty, they could not resist fooling around—first they practised saluting, then they took it in turns to act the chief of staff going in while the other saluted. When one of them saluted, but the other who was taking the part of the chief of staff did not return the salute, they started quarrelling, and the pseudo-chief of staff said, "I'm the chief of staff, I return your salute only if I feel like it!"

"You can't even return a salute. What sort of chief of staff are you?"

Just at this juncture a rickshaw stopped outside the hostel, and the passenger got out. As soon as the two guards saw someone coming, they stopped quarrelling and resumed their positions. They were about to challenge the stranger, when he asked, "Is there anyone in charge inside?"

"Yes!" said one. "The chief of staff is there!" But he had no time to ask where the newcomer was from because, without handing him any card, the stranger squared his shoulders and walked briskly in.

Hsiao-hsi had just rolled a heroin cigarette and was in the act of lighting it when he heard someone coming in, but thinking it was the guard he paid no attention and went on smoking. He had just inhaled a mouthful of smoke when the guest parted the curtain. Hsiao-hsi saw that the newcomer was wearing a silk gown and had a moustache, and was obviously someone of importance, therefore he hastily threw the cigarette and heroin into the opium tray, inwardly cursing the guards. The chief of staff also sat up.

"Which of you is in charge?" asked the stranger.

Seeing that he was taking a lordly attitude, Hsiao-hsi pointed to the chief of staff, hoping to impress the guest with his official title, and said, "This is the chief of staff of Division Headquarters!"

The stranger, however, did not turn a hair. Jerking his head toward the chief of staff, he asked, "Are you the chief of staff?"

"I am," the other replied. "What is your business?"

Without waiting to be asked, the visitor turned round a chair which was by the table, sat down opposite the chief of staff and said, "I've come from Honan Province. Old Huo has made arrangements with my people there, and has written a letter and sent me to fetch the things." So saying he produced from his portfolio a letter one foot long, and gave it to Hsiao-hsi who passed it to the chief of staff, at the same time ordering Tieh-so to serve tea.

The chief of staff opened the letter and saw that Old Huo had already recruited one regiment, and wanted him to notify the army and ask for all necessary equipment—uniforms, insignia and weapons for the officers and men of one whole regiment. He had also listed the names and ranks of all the officers in the regiment, and wanted the headquarters to fill up their certificates of commission.

"Are you the regiment commander?" asked the chief of staff.

"No," said the stranger. "The regiment commander is someone in our group. I'm only working with him."

Holding out the list of names the chief of staff asked: "Which are you?"

The visitor got up and came over, pointed to one name and said, "That's our boss. This is me, for the time being I'm just a staff officer."

"Your surname is Wang?"

"Yes, my name is Wang."

"Where are you staying now?"

"In Cheng Ta Hotel."

"Presently you shall move over to stay here," said the chief of staff. And turning to Hsiao-hsi: "Adjutant Li! Prepare a room for Staff Officer Wang!"

"No need," said the visitor. "This is the first time I have been in Taiyuan, and I want to have a good look round. Staying outside one is freer."

"As you like," said the chief of staff. "But if you want anything, come here and ask Adjutant Li."

"That's very good of you," said Wang. "I don't need anything else, only I find heroin very hard to buy here in Shansi." Then turning to Hsiao-hsi: "Just now I saw you smoking some. Will you please get some for me!" As he spoke he took a five-hundred-dollar bill from his case and handed it to Hsiao-hsi.

"Right," said Hsiao-hsi taking the note. "I can do that for you!" Saying this he got up from the bed and invited him to take his place. "There's still some here. Have a few puffs to be going on with!" And he produced a small paper bag from under the opium tray. The guest, looking quite at home, declined first for appearance's sake, then lay down and started smoking.

Having taken the money, Hsiao-hsi found himself in something of a quandary. "If I send someone else, he won't be able to buy it," he thought, "while if I go myself it will seem undignified, and the stranger may look down on me." After some reflection he decided to send Tieh-so with a letter. He sat down at the table and wrote the letter, then went to the door and called, "Tieh-so, you are to go to Fifth Master's!"

"Where is that?" asked Tieh-so.

"Number Ten, Tientitan," said Hsiao-hsi, handing the letter and money to him. "To buy heroin!"

At that time to buy heroin in Taiyuan was an offence punishable with death, so Tieh-so said, "I don't dare!"

"Idiot!" said Hsiao-hsi in a low voice. "Wearing the Forty-eighth Division insignia and buying the heroin in Fifth Master's house, do you suppose anyone will question you?"

Since as he described it there was no danger, Tieh-so took the letter and money. "Go to the small southern room," Hsiao-hsi told him. "Give the letter to Mr. Chang, ask him to fetch the second wife's mother, and he will understand." Tieh-so agreed and left.

Tieh-so found Number Ten, Tientitan, and pushed at the door, but it was closed. He gave a couple of knocks, and someone inside came out and called, "Who's there?" Then the door opened a crack, a head appeared and asked, "Who do you want?"

"I'm looking for Mr. Chang," said Tieh-so, and handed the letter to the other.

"Wait there," said the gateman, and withdrew. After some time he came back and invited him in.

Sure enough, he was taken to the small southern room. There were a number of people there and Tieh-so asked, "Which is Mr. Chang?"

A thin man over forty sitting at a table in the opposite corner said, "I am. Just wait a bit! The woman from Haitze (Haitze was the name of the village where this old woman lived) has gone to the station." Since she was out Tieh-so had to wait, so he sat on a stool behind the door, idly watching the people in the room.

In the southwest corner of the room was a bed, and in the middle of the bed was a lamp. Two people were lying on the bed: one of them a short, thin-lipped individual, the other a man with deep-set eyes. A third man was sitting by the bed craning his neck like a duck, leaning against the legs of Thin Lips and looking at Deep-set Eyes. Deep-set Eyes was holding a piece of tinfoil from a packet of cigarettes, and a small paper tube of thick carton paper about the size of a finger. He put some heroin on the tinfoil and sat up to bake it over the lamp, then put the small paper tube in his mouth and inhaled the heroin that was baked. They shared this pipe between the three of them. The room was a small one. A small table and two stools to the right of the bed reached up to the right wall. On the table was a brass dish, and in it a sliced water-melon. Sitting on the right-hand stool was a fat man with a square face, wearing a long white gown which was unfastened so that his stomach could be seen. Sitting on the left-hand stool was a young man with his hair parted in the middle, wearing a blue cloth gown which fitted him like a glove, sitting up straight and stiff like a ramrod. These two were facing each other eating slices of melon. Fatty ate big slices, guzzling away with his chin and nose buried in the melon, melon seeds cascading down his chest. Ramrod ate differently. He cut the big slices into small crescents, then picked them up and put his head on one side to bite out a curve, like a rat eating peanuts.

The men on the bed and those by the table were all talking away, but a good deal of what they said was incomprehensible to Tieh-so. It was impossible to tell when the conversation had started. The first thing he heard after he sat down was Ramrod saying to Fatty: "The most important thing is to return to the group. Even now I haven't succeeded in returning to my group."

"Doesn't matter," said Fatty. "If you come from the right place and can walk, it's very fast. As for returning to your group, I should have returned to mine for the last two years, but I still haven't. But if I wait my turn I shall have to wait till after 1961, and what use is that?"

"Listen, you!" said Deep-set Eyes to Duck Neck. "Everybody's talking about returning to their groups! What about us?"

"We've never studied," said Duck Neck. "We needn't bother about that!" Then everybody laughed.

"Yours is a quick way," said Fatty to the people on the bed. "You need only go to the secretary's office and register a few times, and you're all right."

"Your way may be slower," said Thin Lips, "still, whenever you are given jobs it's as county magistrate or section chief. But we can only be tax collector or supervisor."

"What does that matter," said Deep-set Eyes, "as long as there's money in it!"

"So long as the secretary general will back us up," said Duck Neck, "nothing else matters! Fifth Master didn't go to school, but isn't he Section Chief of the Civil Affairs Bureau? And Third Master came out of the home university too (*i.e.*, he had attended no school), but isn't he county magistrate of Huaijen?"

Hearing a reference to Third Master, Tieh-so wondered if it was the same one, and asked: "Which Third Master?"

"Which Third Master?" Duck Neck looked at him superciliously. "How many Third Masters do you think there are in this county?" So Tieh-so held his peace.

Ramrod was speaking again, saying that belonging to a group was still the important thing. "You are too conservative," said Fatty. "Now Hopei has fallen, there are plenty of jobs going. You'd better take my advice and take the train to Peking tomorrow. Once there, if we can only find the secretary general, there will be no difficulty at all for us both to get jobs as county magistrates...."

"I don't believe you can get proper jobs without joining a group," put in the Ramrod.

"You may have joined a Shansi group," said Fatty, "but what use is that once you get to Hopei? And since you can only join an optional group, what use is that? Unless you have connections, you still won't get anywhere."

As they were arguing the door opened to admit several more people. First came a big man with a bushy beard wearing glasses, who greeted the two by the table as soon as he came in. When he saw there was still some melon on the table he started eating, inviting his companions to help themselves too. And with his mouth full of melon, he asked: "What are you two arguing about?"

Fatty started telling him what Ramrod had said about joining a group. The man with glasses cut him short, saying: "Rubbish! This really is a time when jobs are going begging. If we can only find the secretary general, even a broomstick with a hat on could be a county magistrate! Don't talk about optional groups or any other groups! We shall form a grabbing group!"

When he said this they all burst out laughing, and said, "We've joined a grabbing group!"

Although Tieh-so knew nothing about groups, he understood that they were looking for jobs. While he was watching them bellow with laughter someone nudged him from behind, and said, "Isn't it Tieh-so?" He looked round to see Chun-hsi, who had come in with the man in glasses. Seeing that it was indeed Tieh-so, Chun-hsi asked, "Have you joined the army too?" But before Tieh-so could answer him, he had disappeared behind some others and squeezed his way to the bed. "Let me ride the aeroplane too (a collo-quialism for smoking heroin on tinfoil)," he said to Duck Neck. Then he took a paper packet from his little straw hat, and squeezed onto the bed.

The man in glasses said to Mr. Chang: "Go and see if Fifth Master has finished writing that letter to Section Chief Wang of the Army Supply Office." Then Mr. Chang went out.

"Has he introduced you to the Army Supply Office?" asked Ramrod.

"No," said the one in glasses. "The secretary general sent a telegram summoning us to Peking, but because it's difficult to buy tickets we mean to borrow the Army Supply Office's special coach to go."

"Can you take one or two extra?" asked Fatty.

"Afraid not!" said the man in glasses. "Just ourselves makes nearly thirty people! If it's only you it might be managed, but more would be impossible."

While he was speaking Mr. Chang had come back with the letter. The man in glasses took the letter, and left with the people he had come with, Chun-hsi wrapping up his heroin as he hurried out.

Fatty ran to the door and called out: "I shall certainly want a place!"

"Right!" answered the man outside. "But only for one or two!"

When they had gone Mr. Chang asked Tieh-so, "How come you know him?"

"We're from the same village," said Tieh-so.

"He's very capable," said Mr. Chang. "He made a lot of money in the Tax Office at Tatung. The secretary general thinks a lot of him and when he sent this telegram summoning several dozen people, he was included. He only came back yesterday by train from Tatung."

By now the second wife's mother had returned from the station, so Tieh-so bought the heroin and went back, completing his errand. When they had seen off the stranger from Honan, the chief of staff at once prepared an official letter to be sent to the Army Headquarters, and asked Hsiao-hsi as his deputy to fill up the certificates of commission and have insignia made.

4

A FEW DAYS LATER THERE WAS A RUMOUR OF A DEFEAT
in Shantung, and Nanking's aeroplanes came again
to bomb Taiyuan. Panic seized the city, and Shansi
notes depreciated. After a few more days the Army
Headquarters ordered the Forty-eighth Division Headquarters not to enlist men for the time being, and
naturally did not issue any of the equipment requested. The chief of staff passed this order on
to the visitor from Honan, and sent Hsiao-hsi to
northern Honan to recall Old Huo. The headquarters
kitchen was done away with, the guards were dis-
charged, the chief of staff's visits stopped and Hsiao-
hsi himself left. Tieh-so was instructed to go every
day to the chief of staff's lodgings for a fifteen-cent
living subsidy, and to stay in the headquarters as
doorkeeper. To begin with fifteen cents a day was
enough to live on, but later the Shansi currency
depreciated so fast that fifteen cents could only buy

a catty of rice cake; yet when he asked for an increase the chief of staff said: "You go and look for a job! There's no need for a doorkeeper there!" And so the headquarters was abolished.

Tieh-so had acted as bodyguard for a month without receiving a cent of his pay, because after Hsiao-hsi left the chief of staff would not look after him. Now all he had left was a uniform which he dared not wear or sell, but had to take off and wrap up. "In any other jobs it's certain I shan't wear a uniform," he thought. "I'll put it away for the time being, and later if someone asks me for it of course I can ask for my pay, while if no one asks for it it can be made over into civilian clothes." When he had wrapped up the uniform he went back to look for the workmen with whom he had come. They had recently found work. Since Nanking's aeroplanes had started bombing Taiyuan all substantial citizens were hastening to have shelters made, and paid a Shansi dollar a day. When Tieh-so found them he went with them to a certain Chou family to build a shelter, going back to the county hostel at night to sleep.

One evening when he was walking back from work, he saw a crowd of soldiers and civilians blocking the street. His attention was attracted by some people wearing rather outlandish dress and speaking with an accent rarely heard in Taiyuan. There were guards in the streets too, so it looked as if something had happened. When he went back to the hostel he found it crowded. The door of the headquarters was open, and Chun-hsi, with the entire group of people who had been going with him to Peking that day, was there. The bed and floor were packed, his own things being piled up in one corner. As soon as Chun-hsi saw Tieh-so, he said: "Are you staying here? You'll have to find somewhere else today; there are too many of us!"

Tieh-so knew it was no use protesting, so he prepared to move his things out. "Which is Hsiao-hsi's room?" Chun-hsi asked.

"He's gone to Honan," said Tieh-so. "How is it you are all back?"

"We're all back!" said Chun-hsi. "Even Commander Yen has come back!" Tieh-so still did not understand why they had come, but did not care to ask again, so he moved out his things and went back to find his mates.

There were a great many people doing the same work. In addition to those he had come with, he had made the acquaintance of several dozen others, all of whom lived in Manchu Tomb, a street outside the New South Gate. All the houses in this district were small square buildings looking like boxes from a distance. They all had mud floors and leaked badly when it rained; some of them had brick beds, but in others there was just straw spread on the ground. The rent was cheap and was reckoned at so much per head instead of so much per room, each person paying fifty cents a month. Tieh-so moved into a long narrow courtyard with four houses in a row. The east house consisted of a single room in which two students lived, while the three other houses, of three rooms each, were occupied by workmen. He arrived there just as the workmen were having a meal. Holding their bowls of millet, they had gathered round a young student and were listening to what he was saying. This student was about twenty years old. He was wearing a red sleeveless jacket, and over it a blue uniform. He had strong brown arms, a thick mop of hair, and eyes that twinkled as his glance darted about. He answered the men's questions one by one, telling them the Shansi troops had been defeated and both Yen Hsi-shan and Wang Ching-wei had retreated to Taiyuan.

"Two sides are fighting for mastery, but why should Nanking's aeroplanes come to Taiyuan to bomb rickshaw men and small peddlers?" asked one.

"We've had a hard time scraping together a few Shansi dollars," said another. "But if they aren't worth anything now, what can we do about it?"

"That's why we must oppose this kind of fighting," said the student. "It doesn't matter who wins, neither side cares about the welfare of the people...."

Tieh-so listened for a while, and though there were things he did not understand, he felt the student was very fair-minded. Having sorted out his things he went out to buy something to eat, and coming back lay down with one of his mates and asked: "Where did that fellow come from who was talking while you were eating?"

"He lives in this courtyard too," said the other. "He goes to San Tsin High School and his surname is Chang. I don't know what the rest of his name is. His classmate calls him Little Chang, so all the rest of us call him Little Mr. Chang, and he doesn't mind; he's really a good sort! He's very friendly to folk like us, and doesn't stand on his dignity at all. He knows what's right and wrong, and he reasons differently from the rest of the gentry."

Recently so many things had puzzled Tieh-so, he had already thought of asking some educated person to explain them; but since they were educated people who did all these queer things, he had not liked to ask. Now, hearing how good this Little Mr. Chang was, he thought of asking him, and said to his friend: "Supposing I went to ask him something, would he answer or not?"

"Of course!" said the other. "He likes talking. As long as you can keep awake he doesn't mind talking half the night!"

"That's good," said Tieh-so, "only I don't know him."

"That doesn't matter," said his friend. "He doesn't care about things like that. If you want to go, I'll take you."

"Fine," said Tieh-so. "Let's go now." So the two of them went over to the east house to see Little Chang.

When they went in Little Chang had already lit a lamp and was sitting by the table, while his classmate was lying on the bed. The workman introduced Tieh-so to Little Chang, saying: "Little Mr. Chang, this friend from my district has some questions he'd like to ask you, is it all right?"

Little Chang's glance swept the two of them, and came to rest on Tieh-so. "Certainly!" he said. "Sit down!" So Tieh-so sat down opposite him. Seeing how neat and competent Little Chang looked, Tieh-so felt it was presumptuous to want to talk with him and did not know how to begin. Observing his shyness

Little Chang said, "We're living together, so we're just like one family. Go ahead and say whatever you like!"

"There are some things that puzzle me," said Tieh-so, "and I want to ask about them; only it's a long story, and once I start it will take a long time."

"Never mind," said Little Chang. "We're living in the same place. If you can't finish today there's always tomorrow! No need to set a time limit, just see how far you can get."

"Then I'll start from the beginning," said Tieh-so after a moment's reflection. Thereupon he explained where he was from, how he had lost his property at home and come to Taiyuan, and what he had seen and done since, right up to that very evening when he had moved his things over from the hostel. When he had recounted all his experiences he said: "There are so many things I don't understand. Why doesn't Li fall? Third Master behaves so wickedly, yet instead of being punished why does he get given official jobs? How do people like Hsiao-hsi and Chun-hsi always get away with it? Other people are executed for selling heroin, why is an exception made for Fifth Master's house? When a bandit chief arrives, instead of being arrested why is he treated as a guest of honour? How can a division commander go to make friends with bandits?..."

Before he had finished his questions Little Chang started chuckling and came over to slap him on the back, saying, "You've seen through them all right, friend! That's what the world is like nowadays, there's nothing strange about it!"

"Do you mean that the people over them have no sense of right or wrong?" asked Tieh-so.

"Exactly!" said Little Chang. "If the people above didn't set the example, they wouldn't dare act that way."

"If the world is like that," said Tieh-so, "what hope is there in life for people like us who are always the underdogs?"

"Of course we can't allow things to go on like this forever," said Little Chang. "Eventually these unprincipled warlords will be beaten; and when honest people like ourselves take over there will be some justice in the world."

"Who can beat them?" asked Tieh-so.

"If we can work together," said Little Chang, "those bad people are in the minority."

"How can we work together?"

"There is a way," said Little Chang. "It's too late today, tomorrow I'll tell you all about it." Tieh-so listened, and the whole courtyard was quiet, the friend who had brought him having long since gone back to sleep. So he took his leave and went back to bed.

It was a long time, however, before he could sleep. Little Chang struck him as a strange person. All the educated people he had seen treated common folk like himself as a shopowner treats his assistants, only speaking to them to admonish them, encouraging them if they did anything good and blaming them if they did anything bad, but none of them had ever treated him as an equal. Little Chang was the first to treat him as a friend. As for what Little Chang had said, he agreed entirely. He too felt the world would be no good until these unjust people had been overthrown and their place taken by just people; but he did not know how this could be done, and would have to wait till the next day to find out from Little Chang. That evening he was happier than he had been for several years. · Since the world contained someone like Little Chang, it could not be such a bad world after all.

The next day as he worked he thought of Little Chang, and the time dragged till evening when he laid down his tools in the shelter and climbed out. On the road home he did not stop once, but hurried straight back to Manchu Tomb, and went straight to the small east house to look for Little Chang. Little Chang was not there, but cases and books were scattered in disorder on the floor and Little Chang's classmate was there putting together his things.

"Hasn't Little Mr. Chang come back yet?" asked Tieh-so.

"Little Chang has been arrested by Garrison Headquarters."

"Tieh-so stared in bewilderment, then recovered from his stupefaction to ask: "Why?"

Little Chang's classmate looked at him, and muttered: "Who knows?" Having said this he moved out his things. Tieh-so felt he could not question him any further, and, following him out, watched him call a rickshaw and leave. By this time all Tieh-so's mates had come back from the streets, and when he told them what had happened they rushed into the small east house to have a look. The silent tables and stools were still in their places, the floor was strewn with odds and ends of paper, but the inmates were gone.

Nobody could understand what had happened. They were all puzzled. An old carpenter who had been a long time in Taiyuan said: "He must be a Communist. These last few years they have caught a lot of Communists, and killed quite a few of them! It's really a shame! They're all smart youngsters in their twenties."

"Who are the Communists?" asked Tieh-so.

"I'm not quite sure," said the old carpenter. "I've heard they're always against the present officials, and disapprove of these bandits!"

"He probably is," said another.

"Little Chang didn't talk like those officials."

"Little Chang really talks sense."

After discussing it for a long time they agreed it was a shame this should have happened to someone like Little Chang. Many of them took it so much to heart that, although the same amount of millet was prepared as the previous day, half a pan was left uneaten.

Tieh-so ate only half a bowl of millet. Little Chang seemed to be the only good person in the world, yet he had only known him for a day and now he was gone. Hearing what the old carpenter said about Communists and how such people were often killed, he thought: "Since many of them have been killed, Little Chang can't be the only one.... Are there still many left?" And again: "If many of them have been killed, does that mean Little Chang will be killed? If a young fellow like that, so able and reasonable,

who was talking so cheerfully yesterday evening, is today taken alive and killed, it's too bad...." Thinking like this, his tears started falling. That night he
was unable to sleep a wink, and he went again to question the old carpenter, but the old man could not tell
him any more.

After that evening, he felt life in a world like this
really was not worth living, and though he went on
building shelters every day he went about his work
listlessly. Sometimes he thought he ought to go home,
but if he went home it would still be the same.

So the autumn passed. Air-raids continued and many families built underground shelters, but the Shansi currency depreciated from day to day, and Tieh-so's group lost interest in the work and gradually scattered to their homes. Later Yen Hsi-shan resigned and went to Dairen. Hsu Yung-chang became garrison commander to maintain order, Nanking's planes stopped coming, and the big households stopped building shelters. When this happened Tieh-so and two or three others who had not yet left found themselves without a job, so had to make plans to go home.

Tieh-so discussed the problem with two of the mates who had come with him. They had heard that the roads were very bad for travelling. Troops had occupied Tsinhsien and Tsincheng. There were disbanded soldiers everywhere who said they were inspecting the roads, but if they came across money in their inspection they confiscated it. Each of the workmen had saved over a hundred Shansi dollars in notes, and although each dollar was only worth about fifty cents, even fifty dollars is a lot of money to a workman, so naturally they did not want to have it stolen. Luckily they were all carpenters, so they were able to hit on a good way to hide their money—that was to hollow out their planes, stuff the notes inside, then nail up the bottom again. Having concealed their money like this, the following morning the three of them packed their belongings and set off. But when they reached the New South Gate Tieh-so remembered that he had left a pair of shoes in the county hostel which were only half worn out, and which it would be a pity to leave behind, so he asked his friends to wait for a little while he went in.

His two mates waited about an hour, but he did not come out. A motor-car drove out, and they moved his things out of the way. Soon after, he appeared with another man, saying as he approached, "You must be tired of waiting. Just my luck! The shoes weren't to be found, and I had to act as bodyguard again!" They asked what had happened, and he told them: "Chun-hsi has come back from Tatung, where he went to get his things. Now he is leaving with a number of other people by the car of the secretary general who is sending some of his relatives home. And he told me to put their cases on the car for them."

One of his friends, who knew Chun-hsi, asked, "What has he been doing in Tatung? What were the cases?"

"I heard he was in some revenue office," said Tieh-so. "People like him can make money. There were three or four heavy cases."

"You are from the same village," said his friend jokingly, "why didn't you ask for a lift in his car?"

"He wouldn't give me a lift in a hundred years," said Tieh-so. Then pointing to the man who was with him, he said, "This gentleman was busy all day in their place, but he couldn't get in!" His two friends looked at the man who had come out with him. He had a long neck (this was Duck Neck who had been at Fifth Master's house that day), wore a black gown, grey jacket and hat, and carried a green velvet case in his hand.

Tieh-so's remark made Duck Neck feel rather humiliated, so he said by way of explanation: "I couldn't get in, there were too many of them! I'll get a horse on the road, it will be just the same, only a little slower." He deliberately spoke of hiring a horse to maintain his dignity.

Having been in Taiyuan for a good many months, Tieh-so had gained some experience, so he said to Duck Neck: "Sir, we would like to take advantage of your escort. They say the road is rather unsafe. Do you mind if we travel with you?"

"I have friends in all the Shansi regiments we may meet," said Duck Neck. "That will be all right. But if we meet troops from other provinces things will be more difficult, and I shall probably only be able to look after myself." Saying this, he gave an artificial laugh.

Accordingly they set out together. Soon they reached a travelling station where Duck Neck hired a donkey to ride, while the three others trudged along behind with their belongings on their backs.

Duck Neck had hired the short-stage type of donkey, so every three or four miles he had to change; hence it took them four or five days to reach Fenshuiling. Although they met several "inspectors" on the road, these treated Duck Neck fairly politely, just looking at his passes and letting him go. And when the three others said they were travelling with Duck Neck they were only perfunctorily examined. After they passed Fenshuiling, however, they met two more "inspectors"; and although these were also Shansi soldiers, the case was different this time. They opened up the three men's baggage and searched every piece of clothing: it was lucky their money was hidden and could not be found. When Tieh-so's uniform was discovered he felt apprehensive, but it excited no attention. However, the inspectors confiscated twenty dollars they found in Duck Neck's case.

After this experience they realized Duck Neck was no use, and accompanying him wasted time. They wanted to go on ahead, but felt it would be awkward, so continued as they were. Approaching the village of Tsuitien they came upon more "inspectors" who signalled to them from a distance with their rifles, and shouted "Stop!" The four men began to quake in their shoes, until they saw it was Hsiao-hsi who had called to them to halt. There were two other men in uniform a little farther off.

When Hsiao-hsi saw Duck Neck he smiled and said, "So it's you!" And to Tieh-so, "Are you going back too?" Tieh-so replied that he was, and Hsiao-hsi turned to the two men in uniform and said, "These are our own people!" Then he said to Duck Neck: "It's getting dark; suppose we put up together."

"Where?" asked Duck Neck.

"Let's stay at Tsuitien." Then he said to the two in uniform, "There's nobody on the road now, we'll take our things and go back!" He and the two men ran to the back of a big rock, emerging with a large package each, after which the seven of them set off for Tsuitien. By this time it was already dark. Hsiao-hsi led them to an inn door and called the inn-keeper to open up, ordering him: "Find us a clean room!" The inn-keeper saw this was someone who must be treated with respect; then, looking at Tieh-so and his friends, he asked: "Are you all together?"

"We three are workmen," said Tieh-so. The inn-keeper lit a lamp and showed Hsiao-hsi and the three others to his best room, then showed Tieh-so and his friends to another room.

The other four shouted out orders, demanding this and that. Tsuitien was a small place and the inn-keeper could not meet their requirements immediately, so he was soundly cursed. Finally he found some eggs and made them noodles fried with eggs. Only after he had finished serving them did he set about preparing food for Tieh-so and the other two. By the time they had finished eating it was already midnight.

The room they were in was not far from the centre room, and they could hear the others talking there. Duck Neck was complaining how he had lost twenty dollars that day, and Hsiao-hsi said: "Never mind. Tomorrow you can take some from us."

"It's really too bad," said Duck Neck. "It makes no difference how much one carries! They say between Tsinhsien and Tsincheng they search very strictly!"

"I want to go back too," said Hsiao-hsi. "Tomorrow you come with me, and nobody will search you."

When one of Tieh-so's friends heard this he said softly: "Do you hear? Hsiao-hsi is going back tomorrow too. If we go with him tomorrow it may be better than with Duck Neck, because he's in army uniform, and he's in that business himself."

"If we go with him," said Tieh-so, "we won't have any trouble with 'inspectors,' but I really don't want to be with that lot!"

"It's only travelling with them," said his friend, "not being friendly with them."

After a moment's reflection Tieh-so's common-sense asserted itself. Travelling with Duck Neck that day had been equally uncomfortable, yet they had kept with him; so it did not matter if they joined this group. Besides, he had been Hsiao-hsi's bodyguard for a month, and because of this connection Hsiao-hsi could not well refuse. Thus he decided it did not matter one way or the other.

The next morning Tieh-so and his two friends got up very early, and by the time they had prepared their meal and eaten it, the four men in the centre room were getting up. Presently they heard them quarrelling.

"When there is any profit everyone should share!" said Hsiao-hsi. "You can't take all the silver dollars yourselves and push all the Shansi notes onto me!"

"You won't lose out on this," said a man with a Honan accent. "I only thought since you are a Shansi man you should be able to use Shansi notes; if you ask us to take them back to Honan they won't be the slightest use. All those clothes you've been given are worth several hundred dollars!"

"We've been together for a month," said Hsiao-hsi, "and travelled scores of miles together. In all that time have I taken advantage of you in any way? Now you've got over two thousand silver dollars and some twenty or thirty gold rings. Yet you give me a heap of worthless Shansi notes and some old clothes. Do you feel this is right? If there's any profit let's share it together, just as we've shared trouble. Surely I've risked my life just as you have?"

"Old Li!" said another Honanese. "Don't say any more! We've all been friends together, but meeting as friends is not as good as parting as friends! You take a few of these rings! You'll have to keep the Shansi notes. Take another two hundred silver dollars as well." At this point the inn-keeper brought in fried bread, and they stopped quarrelling to eat. When they had finished eating the two in uniform shouldered their heavy loads, and parted very politely from Hsiao-hsi and Duck Neck. The other two did not escort them out, just nodding to them from the door of their room, then went back in to pack up their things.

At this point Tieh-so's friends urged him to go and speak to Hsiao-hsi about travelling together. As soon as he entered the centre room he saw a great heap of Shansi notes on the bed, two packets of silver dollars, a pile of gold rings and two or three parcels of clothes. Hsiao-hsi was in the middle of sorting the clothes, and seeing him come in said, "Haven't you gone yet?" Duck Neck asked the same question.

"They say the road is very unsafe," said Tieh-so. "We would like to travel with you to have your protection, if we may?"

Hsiao-hsi was in a good mood, and answered cheerfully: "Sure! We'll go together! No trouble at all!" Tieh-so had nothing else to say to him, so just stood there watching him. Seeing he had nothing to do, Hsiao-hsi pointed to the clothes and said: "You straighten these out for me. Then wrap them up well."

Tieh-so regretted that he had not gone straight out, but it was too late. "Did you know him before?" Duck Neck asked.

"He was my bodyguard," said Hsiao-hsi. "He's from my village." Having given Tieh-so the clothes to pack, he occupied himself with sorting out the silver on the bed. Then he divided the notes into piles, picked up one pile (between one and two hundred dollars), and gave it to Duck Neck saying: "Didn't you lose some money yesterday? Take this!"

Duck Neck wanted to decline, but Hsiao-hsi said: "Take it. In unsettled times like these, anything one can get should be shared." He pushed the notes onto Duck Neck's lap, and this time Duck Neck accepted them.

Then Hsiao-hsi turned to Tieh-so and asked: "Do you still have that army uniform?"

Thinking he wanted it, Tieh-so said, "Yes! Presently I'll go and get it for you! Only the chief of staff never paid me any salary."

"I don't want it," said Hsiao-hsi. "You'd better put it on and act as my bodyguard again: that will make travelling easier. And you needn't carry the baggage. When we get to the station we'll hire a porter to carry yours."

"There are two others with me," said Tieh-so.

"Never mind," said Hsiao-hsi. "We'll say they're all my people."

Presently the packing was finished. Tieh-so went out to explain things to his two friends, and put the uniform over his padded clothes. Then he shouldered Hsiao-hsi's pack and the five of them left the inn and went to the travelling station, where Hsiao-hsi said off-handedly to the man in charge: "We need two donkeys, three porters!"

The station master looked out of the window and asked, "Why should carpenters need a porter?"

"You fool!" said Hsiao-hsi. "Aren't there carpenters in the army?"

Tieh-so's two friends outside the window said: "We'll carry it ourselves!"

Hsiao-hsi gave them a look through the window and said, "You carry it then!" And to the station master: "Then that will be two donkeys, one porter." When the station master had provided them, Hsiao-hsi and Duck Neck got on the donkeys, the donkey driver and Tieh-so followed them, the porter came next carrying Tieh-so's belongings and Hsiao-hsi's pack suspended from a pole over his shoulder, and Tieh-so's two friends carrying their own possessions brought up the rear. So this procession of seven men and two beasts left Tsuitien.

Hsiao-hsi's pack was very heavy, and the porter panted as he went. Tieh-so had not at first meant to add his baggage to the porter's load, but since he was Hsiao-hsi's bodyguard he had to obey Hsiao-hsi's orders. Climbing a hill Tieh-so noticed that the porter was panting even more, so went over to him and said: "Aren't you tired? Let me take it for a while."

"You're a good sort," said the porter, "but I don't dare let you take it."

"What does it matter," said Tieh-so. "I can carry it." And he went to take over the load. The porter kept repeating that he dared not, and the donkey driver hurried over to say, "That wouldn't do! I'll take it for him for a bit!" So saying he transferred the load to his own shoulder. The porter took a deep breath and said, "Whew! Good Sergeant! There aren't many good fellows like you about."

"There really aren't," said the donkey driver. "Most people wouldn't dream of helping you with the load. You have to be thankful if they don't beat you!"

While they were speaking some more "inspectors" came into view—one of them in the act of searching two merchants' packs, but when they saw Hsiao-hsi and the others approaching they told the merchants to fasten up their things, and let them go.

Hsiao-hsi on his donkey could see very clearly, but he deliberately called out: "Halt! What regiment are you?" This frightened the soldiers so that they hurried off without turning back.

"Did they take anything?" the porter asked the merchants.

"No," said the merchants, and turning to Hsiao-hsi: "Many thanks, Sergeant. If you hadn't come we should have been in trouble!"

Hsiao-hsi on his donkey shook his head, saying, "Don't mention it—the rogues! What effrontery! Holding up people on the road in broad daylight!"

The donkey driver supposed Hsiao-hsi knew nothing about such things, so staggered forward under his load to say: "Good Sergeant! This is nothing unusual! Goodness knows how many cases there are like that in one day on this road!"

Tieh-so behind him wanted to laugh but dared not, only muttered to himself: "Do you want to explain it to him? Why, that pack you are carrying is made up of things confiscated in 'inspection'!"

By putting on his army uniform again, Tieh-so had landed himself in trouble. All along the road he was responsible for fetching water and food, asking the way and changing donkeys, while Hsiao-hsi and Duck Neck did nothing but issue orders. But although he regretted it, he could not think of a way out, and had to carry on.

After they passed Tsinhsien the road became more level, and by exchanging the donkeys for mule carts, they were able to travel much more comfortably than before. On the day that they passed Tunliucheng it began to snow, and in some places the roads were too muddy for the cart to pass. The mule, unable to pull them across one muddy ditch, stopped, and the carter asked them to get out. But when Hsiao-hsi and Duck Neck saw that getting out would mean walking through the mud, they refused and insisted on his carrying on. The carter gave his mule a couple of lashes with the whip and the mule strained forward, but the cart wheels were deep in the mud and would not move.

"What do you think you are doing?" said Hsiao-hsi. "You can't even drive that beast!"

"Sergeant," said the carter, "we really can't get across."

"You villain!" said Hsiao-hsi, "I'll have you beaten!" And he ordered Tieh-so, "Give him a beating!"

Tieh-so had never struck anyone in his life, and he did not think the carter a villain; so instead of beating him he helped him push the cart. But even so they could not budge it. The carter asked the two passengers again to get down, whereupon Hsiao-hsi seized his whip and struck him on the side of the head; when the carter put his hand up to his ear the second stroke fell on his hand, so that both his hand and his ear were slashed. He started shedding tears, and when he wiped the tears with his fists his whole face was covered with blood. When Tieh-so and his two friends saw this they fairly boiled with indignation, but could do nothing to help him. Even after this beating the cart still would not budge. Finally the carter carried Duck Neck across on his back while Tieh-so carried Hsiao-hsi, after which they were able to get the empty cart across.

That evening when they put up at Paotienchen, Tieh-so said privately to his friends: "Let's not go with them tomorrow! I really can't stand this kind of thing!" His friends agreed with him entirely, but said: "The bandits may rob us if we don't go with them."

After their meal Tieh-so told Hsiao-hsi that he and the other two wanted to go back through the mountains, and Hsiao-hsi said to Duck Neck: "In that case you had better wear uniform tomorrow!" To Tieh-so he said: "All right, but take that uniform off, and give it to him." All Tieh-so wanted at this point was to get away from them, accordingly he took off the uniform which represented a month's work, and gave it to him, and the next day they separated.

Chun-hsi went home by car, Hsiao-hsi with the official escort, but Tieh-so had to travel through the mountains for a few days before he reached home. However, although he and his friends were searched once more on the road, the notes were well hidden and they did not lose them.

Shansi notes had continued to depreciate, until now one dollar was only worth twenty cents. Hsiao-hsi took his Shansi notes to the troops at Tsincheng and changed them for opium, but Tieh-so could not do this. He had to watch the notes depreciating, knowing there was nothing he could do about it. After some time he heard that Yen Hsi-shan had returned to Taiyuan as Pacification Commissioner, and dollar notes had gone up to twenty-five cents. This was the end of the year by the lunar calendar. Old Wang, manager of the grocery shop, supposed that since General Yen was back, the notes would recover their value. So he accepted Shansi notes for the repayment of debts and purchase of goods. But now that Tieh-so could easily get rid of his hundred-odd Shansi notes, the fact that Old Wang was so ready to take them convinced him they must be going to increase still more in value, and he did not want to let them go. So he only took a dozen dollars to buy odds and ends for the New Year. After New Year, however, it was decreed that Shansi notes were worth five cents each. Old Wang was very put out, while Tieh-so was at his wits' end, having worked six months for nothing.

After this Tieh-so finished up all his money by paying the army maintenance tax. This tax was a new way of raising money in this locality. There was no fighting but troops from other provinces stationed in Shansi had to be fed, so every two months Yen Hsi-shan levied an army maintenance tax for them, reckoning one ounce of silver as seven dollars fifty cents each time. Tieh-so was an outsider, and of course the land bought by outsiders was heavily taxed, so although he only had one acre of poor land left he was assessed as if the soil were good, and taxed for .576 of an ounce. Each time the tax was levied he had to pay four dollars thirty-two cents in cash, or eighty-six dollars forty cents of his Shansi notes.

Tieh-so was not the only one who could not pay this tax. With the exception of Li, Chun-hsi and a few other landlords, practically nobody could pay it. Little Mao was village elder, but because he was in arrears with the payment he ran away. Disbanded soldiers kept coming to the village and looking for the village elder, so nobody would take the job until the natives conspired to elect Tieh-so to the post. Once burdened with this responsibility, Tieh-so had no time to cultivate his land or work as carpenter: he was busy day and night collecting taxes.

At this time Yen Hsi-shan issued official opium (the government name for it was "tablets for curing opium addicts" but the common people called it official opium), which had to be sold by the village elder too. Opium smokers like Li could still buy privately from Hsiao-hsi, but he would have nothing to do with the poor addicts who only bought a very small amount at a time, and these had to go to the village elder to buy the official opium. According to custom anyone buying the official opium had to pay hard cash; but although this might be the case in other villages, outsiders like Tieh-so could not afford to offend anybody, so that it was hard to collect payment. Thus, in addition to collecting the army maintenance tax, he had to collect payment for the official opium too. Both were hard to collect, and meantime he had no means of raising his own tax money. When the authorities pressed for the tax money he had to add the opium money, and when they pressed him for the opium money he would use tax money to make up the amount. But he never had enough. So, whatever the authorities asked for, he had to go to Old Wang and borrow money to make up the deficit.

When almost a year had passed like this, the troops from outside the province left, things became a little more peaceful, Little Mao felt the position of village elder was worth having again, and after talking it over with Li the job was taken away from Tieh-so and given back to him. When Tieh-so resigned from office he was over forty dollars in debt to Old Wang, part of this sum being due from the opium addicts. His accounts were about right, but he had not a dollar in hand, so he asked Old Yang and Old Chen to go and talk it over with Old Wang, and persuade him to accept an I.O.U.

6

AFTER TIEH-SO WAS MADE VILLAGE ELDER, THINGS went from bad to worse with him. In the space of three or four years his family was reduced to living from hand to mouth: their clothes had been patched again and again, and they had only cotton clothes for the winter. Although he was a carpenter, people who could afford to hire carpenters were afraid that anyone as poor as he would try to cheat them in small ways, and did not like to hire him. So he could find no work and had to ask for a few handfuls of rice here, a few catties there, never knowing where the next meal would come from.

By 1935 they could not make ends meet any longer, and had to send Little Fatty, now just eight years old, to look after cattle for other people; while Tieh-so and a few other carpenters went further afield to look for work. But this time, having no money to make the journey to Taiyuan, he accompanied the other carpenters to the county seat. In town they found work with the family of the fat man who had eaten water-melon that year in Fifth Master's house and talked of "belonging to a group." His name was Wei and for the last few years he had been a purchasing agent in Yen Hsi-shan's Opium Prohibition Bureau (the headquarters for selling the official opium). Having grown rich by buying opium in Suiyuan Province, he had become one of the foremost of the local gentry, and was hiring workmen now to build a house in town. Tieh-so and the others agreed on the amount of wages with the labour contractor, and started work.

For the first part of this year Tieh-so's family was a little better off; and after the autumn harvest, although by the time they had paid the interest due to Old Wang there was very little grain left, Tieh-so and Little Fatty were both away from home, and Erh-niu by herself needed very little to eat.

Unfortunately, something unforeseen happened. The authorities announced that since Communist troops had crossed the river from Shensi, every district must show redoubled vigilance: it was better to kill a thousand innocent people than let one Communist escape. When the county magistrate received this order, he started acting like a madman. He despatched the Anti-Communist Guard and the police to arrest people right and left—folk who had one or two copper coins on them, one or two threads, small mirrors or anything else out of the ordinary, were accused of carrying these as Communist tokens. Refugees, ginger-vendors, and other small peddlers, as well as strangers to the place, were also arrested and killed daily. One day they killed over one hundred and fifty. The police went several times every night with flashlights to inspect the place where the workmen were staying, and two of the workmen were killed because copper coins were found in their possession. By this time, naturally, they all lived in dread of being arrested; and when Fatty Wei heard that the Communists would kill all like him who had bullied and cheated people, fear made him lose all interest in building. At the same time the weather turned cold and the earth would soon be frozen. For these reasons work was stopped, and Tieh-so and the other workmen dispersed to their different homes. When he reached home he found the village office was also busy organizing an Anti-Communist Guard, and Chun-hsi was village captain of the Righteous Brigade (a body organized by Yen Hsi-shan to suppress the Communists). Hsiao-hsi had been made village captain of the Anti-Communist Guard and was conscripting and training all able-bodied men. As soon as Tieh-so got back he was roped in.

That winter the Shansi troops were kept on the move, and a Kuomintang army was also sent to Shansi to help suppress the Communists: thus there were always troops moving about the countryside. And the country folk, who had been through the troubled times of 1930, were naturally afraid at the mere sight of soldiers.

Old Yang's daughter Chiao-chiao was engaged to Erh-niu's younger brother Pai-kou. She was the youngest daughter, not yet eighteen, but because of the unsettled situation her father could not feel easy about her, so he urged Old Chen to let Pai-kou marry at once. Old Chen thought his grandson at nineteen was old enough to get married. Besides, his family was not well off and they could take advantage of the prevailing disorder to have everything on a simpler scale. So he gave his consent immediately, and the marriage took place on New Year's Eve by the lunar calendar. Although Old Chen was by no means rich and was an outsider, his fair dealing had won him many friends. The villagers knew he could not afford to spend much and they were only able to make a modest living themselves, so they chipped in to buy some dragon-phoenix scrolls for him to give the bride's family. According to the custom of the district, those who gave scrolls like this were entertained with wine but not food, and a little wine will go a long way. After the wedding Old Chen prepared some wine, and just after the lunar New Year, on the third day of the first month, he invited guests.

That evening Tieh-so was in Old Chen's house helping him entertain the guests. After a lively time most of the guests had gone home, leaving only the more intimate neighbours like Leng-yuan or relatives from the country. Because this was New Year nobody was busy, so they went on sitting round the table finishing up the pot of wine that was left and chatting. After talking of this and that, they started discussing the business of resisting the Communists, and Leng-yuan said to Tieh-so: "Hsiao-hsi keeps telling us that the Communists kill people just like cutting grass, but nobody has actually seen such cases. You've been around, and visited Taiyuan—did you see any cases?"

This question loosened Tieh-so's tongue. Since his return from Taiyuan he had been too busy and too poor to have a heart-to-heart talk with the others. All that he had to say had gone unsaid. Ever since he had met Little Chang four or five years ago, he had not forgotten him for a single day, always considering him as the best person in the world. And whenever anything he disapproved of happened, he remembered how Little Chang had said: "We've got to overthrow all these unjust bullies and let fair-minded people like ourselves take charge before the world will become a proper place." That year the old carpenter had said Little Chang was a Communist and that Yen Hsi-shan had been killing Communists ever since 1927, so he thought Communists must be people like Little Chang. Unfortunately, after that he had heard no more about such things for five or six years. Then, when he was in town, he heard that the Communists had crossed the river, and thought exultantly that the time had come when all those bullies would be overthrown. But when he saw how many people were being killed in the county and how the army was moving from place to place, he realized that to overthrow them was not going to be an easy business, because the bullies were in power and had the advantage of their official position.

However, his outlook had changed. Five or six years earlier he had felt there could not be many people like Little Chang and nothing would be done.

Now, having heard that the Communists had been able to fight their way across the Yellow River and occupy quite a few counties, and having seen how panic-stricken the bullies were, he felt the Communists were gaining in strength, and although they could not overcome the authorities right away, in a few years they would be more powerful, for Little Chang had said: "If we can work together, those bad people are in the minority." He had declared too that there was a way to make people work together; the pity was that before he could explain it he had been arrested. Tieh-so was sure that the people who had fought their way across the river must understand this way, and once they came to this village they would be sure to explain it to everyone. Through a hard winter these convictions had kept his spirits up, so that whenever he heard Hsiao-hsi or Chun-hsi condemn the Communists he just smiled to himself and thought: "When the Communists come, they'll kill all of you bullies! Let's see how much longer you can lord it over us." However, thoughts like these Tieh-so had kept to himself. But Leng-yuan's question this evening made him feel he must get all this off his chest. Besides, it was New Year and they were all friends, and he had been drinking more than he should, so he was eager to talk.

"I met one," he said, "but it's a long story. Sure you want to hear it?"

They had been harangued by Hsiao-hsi and Chun-hsi for several months without seeing a single Communist, so of course they wanted to hear. "Go on!" they said. "We've nothing to do tomorrow, it doesn't matter if we go to bed a little late."

Leaping up to squat on his chair, Tieh-so poured himself another cup of wine and drained it. Then, straightening himself and raising his head, he proceeded to describe all that had happened to him in Taiyuan. In all his twenty-seven years Tieh-so had never been as happy as he was this evening. He spoke succinctly and to the point, and his listeners, although they had heard many gentlemen talking, felt none of them was equal to Tieh-so. He told of all the civilian and army officers he had met at Taiyuan—such as the chief of staff, Hsiao-hsi, the bandit visitor from Honan, Thin Lips, Duck Neck, Deep-set Eyes, Fatty, Ramrod and the rest, and it sounded like a novel as he gave the details, chapter and verse. When he came to how he met Little Chang at Manchu Tomb, he repeated word for word what Little Chang had said to him, so that his listeners felt they could see it all with their own eyes. And when he described how Little Chang had been arrested, Tieh-so was not the only one to break down—they all shed tears. Only at the very end did he tell them: "An old carpenter said Little Chang was a Communist."

When he finished, everybody was very pleased. They were tired of hearing Hsiao-hsi describing how the Communists killed everybody at sight and burnt all the houses they saw, and already some of them were sceptical: it seemed hardly possible that there could really be people interested only in killing others. Now they had received additional confirmation that Hsiao-hsi and the rest were simply spreading rumours.

"From what you say," said Leng-yuan, "the Communists do good things! In that case, why do we have to resist them?"

Without giving Tieh-so a chance to speak, someone answered for him: "Don't you realize that the ones who organize the resistance all belong to that gang? Like the chief of staff, Third Master, Fifth Master and the people in Fifth Master's house whom Tieh-so described. And like Sixth Master who lends eighty instead of a hundred, or our village head, or Hsiao-hsi and Chun-hsi. Naturally they want to resist the Communists, because as long as the Communists don't come they are masters, but once they come they'll lose their authority. Of course they oppose them!"

"If you put it that way," said Leng-yuan, "by joining the Anti-Communist Guard aren't we acting as their watch dogs?"

"Yes, of course!" Everybody burst out laughing.

They had talked so long that it was already midnight, so they all went home.

The villagers who had heard Tieh-so became convinced that the Communists were good, and although they were so strictly watched that no one dared praise the Communists openly, still, everybody has close friends: one person told ten, ten told a hundred, and in a very few days all decent folk in the village realized that Hsiao-hsi, Chun-hsi and the rest were out to deceive them. Fortunately, Hsiao-hsi and Chun-hsi knew nothing of this talk, aware only that the men in their Anti-Communist Guard were becoming increasingly slack.

"The Communists only fight rogues like Hsiao-hsi, they don't kill the people." Eventually this news spread so widely that Hsiao-hsi and the others got wind of it and began making enquiries. But everybody said it was just talk that was going about, nobody knew where it had come from. Unfortunately, Leng-yuan's reckless way of talking caused trouble again.

Old Yang's daughter Chiao-chiao was a very pretty girl, and after her marriage she dressed so neatly and looked so charming, she gained the reputation of being the best wife in the village. Hsiao-hsi was a philanderer, and no respecter of persons. If the wife in any family was good-looking, he would go there to pass the time whether he had a pretext or not: so after Chiao-chiao's marriage he was always hanging round Pai-kou's house. Pai-kou was young and could do nothing about it, while Old Chen dared not offend Hsiao-hsi; so whenever he came they just went on with their work in silence, until he was tired of sitting there and left.

One day when Leng-yuan was there and heard how contemptible Hsiao-hsi was, he exclaimed, "Why are the Communists so long in coming? Didn't your brother-in-law say they would kill rogues like Hsiao-hsi?"

Just at this point Hsiao-hsi came into the courtyard, but hearing Leng-yuan's remark he turned on his heel and left again.

Hsiao-hsi went back and told Chun-hsi. Chun-hsi had recently been reprimanded by the local commander because there had been too little to show in the work of resistance, so now he sat down at once and wrote up a report of what Leng-yuan had said, thinking this would be counted to his credit. The local commander reported it to the county commander, who in turn informed the county government, whereupon police were sent to arrest Tieh-so.

If this had happened half a year earlier, Tieh-so's number would have been up. But this was the summer of 1936, the Communists had already withdrawn to Shensi and the earlier rabid attacks on Communism had died down. Moreover, the previous winter when this particular county magistrate was massacring hundreds of innocent people, the Communists had posted pamphlets on his door, so that for several nights he could not sleep for fear, after which he became slightly more polite in his dealings with Communists. Hence he dealt with Tieh-so's case comparatively leniently. After questioning Tieh-so he realized that he had had some contact with Communists, but it had been of the slightest; so he could neither execute nor release him. Because the Righteous Brigade demanded evidence of progress from every Anti-Communist Guard in the different villages, practically every village had sent in exaggerated reports, and there were many cases like Tieh-so's. Later the county magistrate received instructions to start a training class for these prisoners where they could be indoctrinated while doing hard labour—the indoctrination consisting of the same old rigmarole Tieh-so had heard hundreds of times from Hsiao-hsi and Chun-hsi.

Realizing that all the "trainees" were simple, honest, hard-working men, the authorities used them as a free labour corps, making them do over a year of hard labour. After the outbreak of the War of Resistance to Japanese Aggression, many people in the provincial capital requested that political prisoners (those arrested because they disagreed with the authorities) be released. Still the government was reluctant to let a single one go. Later, however, when the League for Self Sacrifice and National Salvation was formed to resist Japan, it negotiated with the county government to mobilize the masses, and these prisoners were released.

7

AFTER THE OUTBREAK OF THE WAR OF RESISTANCE, Shansi patriots organized a League for Self Sacrifice and National Salvation (called the Sacrifice League for short), which sent representatives to the different counties to mobilize the masses to resist Japanese aggression. By this time the Eighth Route Army had already reached Shansi and fought many great battles, annihilating the Japanese Itagaki Division at Pinghsing Pass. The Anti-Communist Guard had also been disbanded, so there was no reason why the training camp where Tieh-so was should not be abolished. When this happened the Sacrifice League sent a speaker to the camp to make a simple speech.

"The Kuomintang and Communists are cooperating," he told them. "This kind of anti-Communist training camp should have been abolished long ago, and in future anyone who attacks the Communists will be a reactionary diehard. . . . When you go home you must all join in the anti-Japanese work whole-heartedly." This was the line taken by mass organizers at the beginning of the war. But this audience consisted largely of men who had been arrested and made to do over a year's hard labour simply for careless talk and a reference to Communism, who during the past year had not dared so much as breathe the word "Communist." So this speech made them heave a great sigh of relief, in the belief that the world had changed.

Tieh-so, however, only gave half his mind to the speech, for he was concentrating on the speaker. When the speaker first mounted the platform Tieh-so thought he looked like Little Chang—the thick mop of hair and flashing eyes were the same, while his face, although some six or seven years had passed, had not changed much. And the way he talked was just the same as when Tieh-so first moved into Manchu Tomb and heard him speak in the courtyard. While he spoke, therefore, Tieh-so paid little attention to what he was saying, simply studying his voice and gestures. And the more he saw and heard, the more convinced he was that this was Little Chang. The speech lasted for about an hour, after which the "trainees" went back to put their things together ready to go home. Tieh-so, however, had no time to think of going back inside: he squeezed past the others and hurried after the speaker.

When he caught up with the speaker he wanted to ask him if he were Little Chang, but coming close he saw that the other was wearing a new army uniform while he himself was dirty and in rags, so he felt ashamed. "Supposing it isn't Little Chang, what should I say?" he wondered, and could not bring himself to speak. But then he thought: "If it really is Little Chang how can I let him go like this?" So he followed him out onto the street. It was over a year since he had been outside, but he was in no mood now to look round carefully. He followed the other for some time, then thought: "If I don't ask I shall never know!" So screwing up his courage he hurried forward and blurted out: "Say! Are you Little Mr. Chang?"

The other stopped at once, and turned to look at him with those eyes that seemed to dart lightning. After a second's hesitation he gripped his hand, saying: "Your face looks so familiar, why can't I remember who you are?"

"In Manchu Tomb at Taiyuan...."

Little Chang smiled and said, "Right, right! Aren't you the one who had just moved in? That evening you raised all sorts of questions, didn't you?"

"Yes."

The other gripped his hand more tightly, and said, "Come on, friend! Let's go to my room for a talk!" He took Tieh-so's hand as they walked on together, asking him his name, where he lived, and particulars of his family. And Tieh-so, naturally, asked what had happened to him after he was arrested.

Tieh-so had been locked up to do over a year's hard labour because he had spoken carelessly after drinking. Now, not only was he released, but he heard that even real Communists could not be arrested, and he had found the man he believed was the best in the whole world. Naturally his happiness knew no bounds.

Nodding his head, he kept saying to himself, "This seems something like a proper world again!" And although he was holding Little Chang's hand in his own and walking by his side, he kept turning his head to look at him as if afraid he might vanish. All the noise and bustle of the streets, the big shops, restaurants and taverns, grain market, vegetable and meat stalls, and the jostling crowds, made not the least impression on him. He had eyes only for Little Chang.

Presently they reached the Sacrifice League, and after offering him a bowl of tea Little Chang started asking about conditions in his village. For seven years, ever since his return from Taiyuan, Tieh-so had been nursing his resentment, regretting that he could find no one like Little Chang to talk with. And now that he had found him again he was only too eager to talk. Only, fearing his story would be too long and Little Chang would tire of listening, he started giving a very brief summary. Little Chang, however, pressed him for more details, and in places where he could not understand stopped him to ask for particulars; while when people's names or place names came up, he even asked how they were written so that he could take notes. They talked until noon, when Little Chang kept him to a meal in the hostel, during which he introduced him to five or six other comrades who were staying there. The meal over, Tieh-so went on to explain in detail who was village head in their village, who was captain of the Righteous Brigade, captain of the Anti-Communist Guard, what they did every morning, and why he had been locked up to do over a year's hard labour....

When he had finished, Little Chang said: "We sent a man to your village, but he didn't understand these conditions you describe. There's been a slight change in your village!" As he said this he brought out a report from their representative, and after referring to it said, "The village head is an outsider now, they say he was trained at Taiyuan. Landlord Li has become deputy head. The Anti-Communist Guard has changed into the Anti-Japanese Self Defence Corps, but the captain is still Hsiao-hsi. The captain of the Righteous Brigade is still Chun-hsi."

When Tieh-so heard this he sighed. "Does this mean the power of people like Li, Hsiao-hsi and Chun-hsi can't be shaken?" he asked. "Why do they stick on through all these changes? Didn't you say all those bad people must be overthrown before the world can become fit to live in? Didn't you say there is a way to make the people work together? What a pity you were arrested that day before you could tell me the way. But today I want to hear it!"

Little Chang burst out laughing. "You really are keen, my friend!" he said. "I can tell you the way today. It's nothing strange, simply this: Everyone must be organized. But this is only the outline: later we can discuss the details. This is just the job our Sacrifice League is out to do. We don't just want to hold our own with those rascals—the important thing is to resist Japanese imperialism—but if we don't hold our own with them, most good folk will be so persecuted and downtrodden they will have no heart left to resist Japanese aggression. You can't expect to understand it all straight off. In a few days I shall visit every village in your district, coming to your village first to have a look, and then we can talk things over more fully. You haven't been home for over a year, you go back first to see how things are, and I'll follow in a few days' time."

"Can you tell me how to organize people," said Tieh-so, "so that when I go back I can tell some of my friends?"

Seeing how much in earnest he was, Little Chang replied promptly: "Certainly! The first thing is for you to join our Sacrifice League!" So saying he gave him a copy of the constitution and a membership form, and after explaining them to him asked if he could write or not. Tieh-so replied that he could not write well, whereupon Little Chang filled out the form for him, after which he handed it to him to read, asking if he had written correctly or not. Tieh-so approved everything, and gave it back to Little Chang to put away.

"This is the way to enlist members," said Little Chang. "When there is any work to be done we all hold a meeting, and when we have decided what is to be done everybody has to help: this is what is meant by organization." Then he gave him a few more copies of the constitution, saying, "When you go back you can ask some of the people you think are really sound if they would like to join the league. If anyone wants to, you can act as his sponsor. The representative we sent is named Wang. He is still working in that area, and if anyone wants to join the league you can ask him to fill up the form. I'll write to him about it." This was no sooner said than done. He wrote a letter and gave it to Tieh-so.

Only when the sun was setting did Tieh-so take his leave of Little Chang and return to the shambles in which he had lived for more than a year to put his things together. Everybody else had gone and meals had stopped. Only an old quilt and some ragged clothes of his were left scattered on the straw of the bed. By the time he had knotted these together it was dark, and since he had no money to stay in an inn he had to go back to the Sacrifice League and ask Little Chang to put him up for the night. The next morning Little Chang kept him to breakfast, and then he started home.

On the way home he was so happy he felt he must talk, but there was no one to listen. So from time to time he sang snatches from an opera, from time to time threw up his head and shouted: "This is something like a proper world again!" So he covered the twenty-odd miles home. It was harvest time and many of the villagers were cutting rice stalks on the threshing floor, for although the sun was setting they could still see to work; but at the sight of Tieh-so they stopped what they were doing and gathered round to question him. The children told Erh-niu, and she came out to the threshing floor to see him.

Naturally the first news he gave them was: "Little Chang is coming."

Immediately all eyes grew wider, and they demanded as with one voice:

"Is it true?" "Where is he?"

Then he told them how he had met Little Chang in the county seat. To begin with, the only people in the village to know about Little Chang were those who had heard Tieh-so talking in Old Chen's house the third of the first month of the previous year. But after Tieh-so's arrest the news had spread, because everybody wanted to know the reason, and Leng-yuan had repeated what Tieh-so had said that evening. When Chun-hsi knew of this he had Leng-yuan called to the temple and ordered him to repeat it in public, thinking this would furnish proof of Tieh-so's collusion with the Communists, in which case his punishment would be more severe. Instead, however, Leng-yuan's speech had the effect of convincing the villagers that there was at least one good man in the world. So now when they heard that in a few days Little Chang would be coming, they all looked forward eagerly to seeing him.

That evening Tieh-so called on Old Chen to find out what changes there had been recently in the administration of the village. Old Chen told him much as Comrade Wang had reported to Little Chang, only he said that the new village head was a classmate of Chun-hsi's, and although he had received training it simply meant he could give empty talks about resisting Japan and saving the country, but when it came to managing affairs he was exactly like Landlord Li. To all intents and purposes it was the same as if Li were still village head. Of Comrade Wang, Old Chen said, "He's a youngster of sixteen or seventeen, a good speaker, and he can write well too. The only pity is he's so young and inexperienced. He was here for a few days just at harvest time, when we were all so busy we scarcely had time to breathe. But he would choose that time to summon everybody to a meeting. He didn't realize how busy we were, but complained we weren't keen enough."

When Tieh-so told how Little Chang had asked him to come back and organize a Sacrifice League, Old Chen said, "There is one already. I don't see what use it is."

"When was it organized? Who organized it?" asked Tieh-so in surprise.

"It was when that boy Wang came," said Old Chen. "He asked the village head to find him someone who would work with a will for the community. At that busy season all decent folk had no time, so the village head got Little Mao to keep Wang company for half a day. After he had gone, Little Mao told us Wang had asked him to organize a Sacrifice League, and just the day before yesterday he was going from house to house getting a list of names, but I don't know if he has sent it in or not."

When Tieh-so heard this he shook his head, and said, "Who would have thought those rogues could be so tricky! They leave no stone unturned!"

Although he had walked over twenty miles that day, and talked till late in the evening, when he got home he could not sleep. Since his arrest Erh-niu had been to the city three times to ask news of him. The first time she was told he had not yet been sentenced and she could not see him, and the second and third times she was only able to say a few words through a door before they dragged her away; so she had never seen how thin her husband had grown, and had longed only for his early release. Now he had come back a changed man, his hair matted to his head, his face yellow and shrunken, his sleeves ragged as two tattered fans. He looked as grimy as if he had been dipped in oil, and legs, knees, shoulders and thighs showed through his lice-infested rags. To see her husband such a wreck of a man was enough in itself to upset Erh-niu. But when she asked him what it was like in the town, and Tieh-so told her how they had drunk gruel made from rice stored sixty years, slept on straw, carried heavy loads and been savagely whipped, she was so distressed she clung to him and wept. Tieh-so had always been soft-hearted, and although the last few years had hardened him a little, still, he had not seen anyone dear to him for over a year, and his wife's concern made him break down too. When they had dried their tears, Erh-niu described her difficulties during the past year, while finally Tieh-so told her the world was changing and soon they would think of a way to overthrow those scoundrels. So they talked till it was dawn.

8

Poor though she was, Erh-niu liked to keep up appearances, and her clothes although patched and mended were very clean. Now she felt Tieh-so was simply not fit to be seen, and immediately set about washing and patching his clothes. There were a great many holes and no cloth to patch them with, so he had to get into bed and wait.

Erh-niu took the clothes to the river to wash, leaving him alone at home. When neighbours dropped in he had to talk to them from the bed, and when they left he started thinking again. "Little Chang said we must organize the good people," he thought. "Rascals like Little Mao are only flunkeys of those rogues, so no good can come of their being included in the organization."

He still had the letter Little Chang had given him, and had originally planned to look for Comrade Wang first thing; but now it seemed Comrade Wang was no use, so he decided to leave him for the time being. He was not going to help Little Mao organize a Sacrifice League in the village, because he wanted to have nothing to do with him; and his best course, he concluded, would be to go back to the county seat to report all these matters to Little Chang. At noon Leng-yuan and some others, bringing their own food, came to chat with him, and when he spoke of a Sacrifice League being organized, they agreed with him: "Better think of a way to keep clear of Little Mao and that lot, otherwise outsiders may not understand what we are up to." This strengthened his resolve to go to town to consult Little Chang, and he decided to leave the next day, when his clothes would be mended.

The weather was cold and the clothes took some time to dry, so it was afternoon when Erh-niu finally brought them home to mend. And they were so ragged that by supper-time she had only finished mending the jacket. At this point Old Sung, the temple custodian, arrived to announce that an envoy of the Sacrifice League had come to the temple looking for Tieh-so.

"Is it some one of twenty-five or twenty-six," asked Tieh-so, "with a thick mop of hair and eyes that sparkle, wearing a grey army uniform?"

"Yes," said Old Sung.

At once he sat up in bed and said to Erh-niu, "Little Chang has come! Hurry up and give me my clothes!"

"Is he Little Chang?" asked Old Sung.

"Yes!" said Tieh-so.

Seeing that he had no clothes on, Old Sung said: "You come when you're ready. I'll go back first to look after him." And he went out.

Erh-niu gave Tieh-so the lined jacket she had already mended, but picking up his ragged trousers she said: "These are really not fit to be seen in, just wait while I borrow a pair of Pai-kou's trousers for you!" So saying she hurried out. Although Old Chen's house was not far, still it took a few minutes to get there, and to find a pair of Pai-kou's trousers of course Chiao-chiao had to look through her cases. Meanwhile Tieh-so was so eager to see Little Chang that after a short wait he grew impatient, and putting on his ragged trousers went out. By the time Erh-niu came back with the borrowed trousers he had already reached the temple.

Although the trousers had not arrived in time to be worn, the news of Little Chang's arrival had been spread—Chiao-chiao told Pai-kou, Pai-kou told Leng-yuan. And once any news was known to Leng-yuan, it spread like wildfire. Presently the whole village knew, and the moonlit street was filled with folk asking each other: "Is it true?" "Has he come?"

When Tieh-so reached the temple he saw that the lamp had been lit in the village administration office, and the village head, Chun-hsi and Little Mao were there entertaining Little Chang. They had finished their meal and tea was being served. When Tieh-so saw them sitting there together he stood by the door just as in the past. Naturally the village head and the other two did not move, but Little Chang stood up and invited him to be seated, whereupon Tieh-so moved very sheepishly to the bench where Little Mao was sitting.

"This is a commissioner from the county Sacrifice League," said Little Mao. "Don't you think you should bow to him?"

Little Chang smiled slightly and said: "We're old friends!" And saying this he grasped Tieh-so's hand, and made him sit down. In such circumstances Tieh-so was tongue-tied, while the village head and the others, seeing that a common peasant so far beneath them had joined them, naturally did not feel like talking either. For a while, then, the whole group was silent, and all that could be heard was a murmur of voices outside the window.

"What are you doing out there?" shouted the village head. Then the people outside ran noisily out of the temple.

Seeing this was no place for the common people, Little Chang said to Tieh-so: "I'd like to visit your home!" Tieh-so, of course, was only too willing, and led him out. When they reached the temple gate the villagers who had been chased away by the village head were still standing there, and made way for them. And when they had passed through, the others followed along behind, as if they were going to watch New Year festivities.

When they reached Tieh-so's gate, Tieh-so invited Little Chang in, but seeing how many people there were he said, "Let's sit outside." And he sat down on the millstone. The onlookers crowded round— women and children, and old people—everyone seemed to be there. One child was crowded onto the millstone, and stealthily fingered the leather strap on Little Chang's back. Leng-yuan saw Little Mao edging his way in, so he called out for all to hear: "All gather round! *This* meeting is open to all!" Then everybody roared with laughter, and Little Chang was impressed by Leng-yuan's ready tongue.

"That was Leng-yuan speaking," Tieh-so whispered, "the one I told you about who likes to talk recklessly."

Then everybody nudged Leng-yuan, saying in low voices, "Go on!" And they passed him from hand to hand up to the millstone.

Leng-yuan said to Tieh-so, "Everybody's heard that Mr. Chang is a very good speaker, so we all want you to ask Mr. Chang to speak for us!"

Tieh-so introduced Leng-yuan to Little Chang, who shook hands with him. Then Leng-yuan said directly to Little Chang: "Will you talk to us, Mr. Chang?"

Little Chang felt it was a fine opportunity for a talk, only he was afraid the villagers had not yet had their evening meal; yet if he asked them to come back after eating they might lose interest, so he decided just to speak for a quarter of an hour. Having made up his mind, he answered Leng-yuan: "Certainly! Let's have a talk!" He saw a platform for sieving rice, and climbed onto it. The villagers had not yet acquired the habit of clapping, but seeing him standing there they said softly to each other: "Hush! Be quiet! Listen!" Immediately everyone was quiet, and he started speaking.

"Villagers! This is the first time I've come here, and so far I only know Tieh-so here, who has been my friend for six or seven years. But now that I've come here I don't feel like a stranger: we are friends as soon as we meet—just as Tieh-so and I became friends as soon as we met! Since my friends want me to speak, I'd better explain what I have come for. I'm a commissioner of the county Sacrifice League, come to organize a Sacrifice League here. The league's name is The League for Self Sacrifice and National Salvation, but because that's too much of a mouthful, we call it the Sacrifice League. Do you all know why we have to save the country?"

Someone answered, "Yes! Because the Japanese have invaded our country."

"For several months," continued Little Chang, "I expect you know all about it, so I won't say much on that. To 'Fight Japan to save China' is the business of all of us. We should set about it together: 'Those with money give money; everybody give strength!' In the past the rich were not willing to give their money, only trying to squeeze money from the poor. That was wrong, because to save the country is the business of all of us, and if the Japanese come the rich people will suffer even greater losses. So we shouldn't ask the masses to be responsible for guarding the door while the rich people only sleep— strength is supplied by all, the rich have got to supply money."

Some people said softly: "He's got the right idea."

"As for everybody supplying strength," continued Little Chang, "this can only be effective if we organize. But organizing is not at all easy. Judging by empty names, Shansi was organized long ago; every village has its Mobilization Committee, Self Defence Corps, Transport Corps, Medical Corps, Women's Sewing Corps, Youth Anti-Traitor Corps, Aged Praying Corps—the records of members' names are enough to fill several carts. But I ask you, have all these organizations really accomplished anything?"

The villagers laughed, because they had long since realized the futility of all these organizations.

Little Chang went straight on: "All these organizations are absolutely useless. Effective organization means getting together to do a real job. Why haven't we done this in the past? There are two reasons, namely that the great majority of people have no money and no power. Without money they have not enough to eat or wear, much less save the country. Take the case of Tieh-so: look at the holes in his trousers! Resisting the Japanese is important, but one can't say that trousers are not important. If we want to send him off to resist the Japanese, we shall first have to think of a way to get him trousers to wear.

"Without power people feel that affairs of the state are none of their business, so they have no interest in saving the country. I don't know about the rest of you, so I'll take the case of Tieh-so again: because he said a few careless words the authorities shut him up to do over a year's hard labour. If his country treats him like this, how can he possibly love his country? After all, a country is like a company in which everyone has shares; but if a few people get control of the shop and deny that all the others are shareholders, what reason do the others have to love and protect the shop? It's not because people are lazy that they have no money. They toil all the year round, but after a year's hardship the money they make is appropriated by the others, who demand grain, contributions, taxes and interest, and cheat them out of many other things too, until what is left is not enough for a pair of trousers.

"It's not because people are no good that they don't have power; it's because the others who seize power beat, punish, kill, arrest and shut them up to do hard labour, until they are completely cowed. If we want to mobilize everyone to resist the Japanese, we must first see that they have money and power. If we want everybody to have money we must cut down taxes and interest, impose only a reasonable burden, settle old debts and improve the livelihood of the masses. If we want everybody to have power we must abolish the special privileges of a few, protect the people's freedom and practise democracy. These are the principles of our Sacrifice League, and our aims in organizing the league. As to how we should organize ourselves to carry out these aims, I can't explain that in full right away; but I shall still be here tomorrow, and if you want to hear we can talk at greater length tomorrow."

The fifteen minutes' talk was at an end, and what had impressed everybody most was that trousers were needed to resist the Japanese, and power was needed to save the country. As for the questions of how to cut down taxes and interest, introduce reasonable taxation and realize democracy, these would have to wait till the next day. Although the speech had been so short, the villagers were well satisfied, and scattered to their homes saying: "That fellow really knows what he's talking about. . . . He talks quite differently from those men sent by the yamen before."

Erh-niu had been so busy listening that she had let a small pan of vegetable soup boil half away. When Little Chang had finished speaking Tieh-so asked him inside, and while they were eating told him of recent developments in the village. Pai-kou, Leng-yuan and a few others specially interested in current events did not go home to eat but gathered in Tieh-so's house to ask all manner of questions. When Tieh-so had described how after Comrade Wang's arrival Little Mao had organized a Sacrifice League in the village, Little Chang said: "Comrade Wang is young, and he doesn't understand conditions in the villages, so he made the mistake of thinking Little Mao was a good person. I can write him a letter and put him wise to this, and next time he comes you can explain the situation in the village to him in detail. As for Little Mao's list of names, we won't recognize it. According to the constitution of our Sacrifice League, anyone joining the league must first understand our principles, then each person must voluntarily find a sponsor and fill up the membership form. Only in this way can he become a member."

"We can refuse to recognize his list of names," said Tieh-so, "but he himself was introduced into the league by Comrade Wang; how can we get rid of him?"

Little Chang laughed and said: "I don't think that will be necessary! Although he used to be a bad lot, still, if he doesn't oppose our principles now, how can we stop him from saving the country?"

"That's no good," interrupted Leng-yuan. "He's just the opposite of us, so of course he opposes our principles. You speak of rich people contributing money, but I know he never will. He's rich, but he's a skinflint, and he joins with Landlord Li to cheat people."

"Well, that doesn't matter," said Little Chang. "Once he has joined the league, we shall ask him to carry out its principles; and if he doesn't carry them out, we can expel him."

Leng-yuan smiled at Tieh-so and said: "That's all right then! In future when there's any need for money, we'll ask him to make a contribution; and if he doesn't contribute we'll have him thrown out of the league."

Pai-kou and the other young men grinned at Leng-yuan and said: "Right! That way we shall always be able to get rid of him!"

Little Chang smiled at them all and said: "Won't you allow him to reform?"

"How could he reform?" said Leng-yuan. "He's too set in his ways."

"But since we admit him," said Little Chang, "we must hope that he will reform. If he really can't, then the only thing is to get rid of him."

The question of whether to admit Little Mao or not was then dropped, and after a few more queries Leng-yuan and the others went home to eat. Little Chang wrote a letter for Tieh-so to take to the district the next morning to Comrade Wang, after which Tieh-so saw him back to the temple to sleep.

Little Mao had heard all that Little Chang said to the villagers, and when the speech was over he hurried to the temple to make a report to the village head and Chun-hsi.

"This shows," said Chun-hsi, "they are against us. Only this Sacrifice League is very powerful just now, so we must make the most of this opportunity to get the league into our own hands. Since you've been in touch with that boy Wang and compiled a list of names, naturally you are the first member of the league in this village, so this evening you report on your work to this commissioner. You must make up to him!"

They plotted for some time how to deal with Little Chang, until Little Chang came back. When Little Mao saw him, he stood up and said deferentially: "Are you back, Commissioner? I was just talking of going to meet you! Old Sung! Serve tea!"

When Old Sung had served tea, Little Mao went on: "Are you tired, Commissioner? You really spoke well! Quite right! The only way to save the country is for everybody to be organized! Ever since I heard Japan had invaded our country I have been seething with impatience, regretting that my strength couldn't be used and that I didn't know what to do to save the country. That day when Comrade Wang of our league came and wanted to find someone enthusiastic who would work for the common good, the village head gave him my name. I can't do much, only I'm willing to run errands and do what I can to help in public business. And since the village head gave my name, I came. As soon as I met Comrade Wang we two saw eye to eye, and Comrade Wang entrusted to me the task of organizing a Sacrifice League in the village. And it is organized already. Only yesterday evening I completed the list of names and was just going to send in a report, and now the commissioner has come!" With this he took from the village head's table his newly compiled list of names and handed it to Little Chang saying, "Commissioner! You look! I've collected quite a few!"

Little Mao's flattering manner and glib speech made Little Chang think: "No wonder Comrade Wang was taken in by him: this rascal really has the gift of the gab." When Little Mao handed him the list of names he took it, but after a cursory glance put it back on the table, saying, "Let's look at it again tomorrow. This evening I'm rather tired!"

Seeing that he did not want to talk any more, Little Mao responded considerately: "Right! You have been travelling, Commissioner, so you should go to bed early! Old Sung! Prepare the commissioner's bed!" And so he left him.

On the other side of the village Leng-yuan and his friends had gathered in Old Chen's house to discuss the work of organization. All without exception agreed with Tieh-so that Little Chang was the best man they had met. "This time let's not make any mistake," said Pai-kou, "but ask him to organize us right away!"

The only thing they did not approve of was Little Chang's assertion that Little Mao could not be forbidden to join the league. "When the time comes for organizing," said one, "if Little Mao so much as says a word we can jump on him. Leng-yuan! You're good at heckling. Mind you heckle Little Mao!"

"We don't dare say anything at ordinary times," said another, "but there'll be plenty of people to heckle him in the meetings! Isn't Pai-kou Leng-yuan's chief disciple?"

"I'm his second disciple," said another youngster.

"I'm his third disciple."

"We must see how things go," said Old Chen, "and not be too rash!"

"Don't you worry," said Leng-yuan. "Didn't you hear Little Chang say that in future everybody would have power? As long as we are within our rights, what can he do to us? I believe the world has already changed to a certain extent, otherwise how could people like Little Chang come here openly to organize us?"

"Right!" said someone else. "Let's be bolder!" They talked together for some time at the top of their voices, all proposing to get a good rise out of Little Mao.

The next morning when Tieh-so went to the district to look for Comrade Wang, Little Chang waited in the temple until, tired of having nothing to do, he started walking about to while away the time. One end of the temple was still filled with images, while at the other end were two large rooms used by the Righteous Brigade and the village administration office. The kitchen was below the platform due south, on the southeast was the main gate, while the southwest room was the headquarters of the Self Defence Corps. Look where he might, he could not see a single room that could be used for the Sacrifice League. There was another small room inside the main gate facing west, but when he looked in he found this was where Old Sung lived. Old Sung asked if he wanted anything, and he said: "Nothing! I was just looking round." And he shut the door after him.

Just then the main gate opened a crack, and a smart-looking youngster poked his head inside. At the sight of Little Chang he started to withdraw, but then he recognized him, and said with a grin: "I thought the village head had come!" Then he opened the door a little wider and came in. This was Pai-kou. Although Little Chang did not know his name, he knew he had seen him—the previous evening when he had finished his speech by the millstone, this was one of the youngsters who had gone into Tieh-so's house and asked all kinds of questions.

"If it had been the village head, wouldn't you have dared come in?" he asked with a smile.

Pai-kou just chuckled.

"Who are you looking for?" asked Little Chang.

"I was looking for you!" replied Pai-kou.

"What do you want with me?"

"To ask when you will speak to us again."

"Is everybody still very busy these days or not?"

"Not too busy," said Pai-kou. "Harvest is over. They all want to hear you speak. If you will only fix a time, it doesn't matter if you talk all afternoon!"

"I'll decide at lunch," said Little Chang, "and when I've decided I'll let you know!" So Pai-kou went away, and Little Chang went back to the office again.

He asked the village head to find an office for the Sacrifice League, and was told there was no room in the temple, but there was another public building in the village where the night watchman had formerly lived, now empty and available. The village head did not want to let the Sacrifice League occupy any part of the temple, fearing that once they moved in he, Li, Hsiao-hsi, Chun-hsi and the rest could not talk freely. Little Chang for his part felt that since the village administration office and Righteous Brigade were in the temple, the villagers would be afraid to go there, for such prejudices cannot be overcome overnight. Moreover it would not be convenient to discuss the village despots there. Since both sides were agreeable, it was decided to use a place outside the temple.

By breakfast time Tieh-so was back, and with him Comrade Wang. They went first to see the proposed building, and having decided to use it, Tieh-so immediately fetched a dozen people to sweep the floor, paper the windows, build up a fire-place, borrow tables and chairs.... Very soon they had the place in excellent shape. Although Little Mao put in an appearance and bustled about to prove his enthusiasm, everybody ignored him, deliberately laughing and joking as if he were not there.

Little Chang and Comrade Wang had a talk about the situation in the village, and Little Chang told him in future if he had any problems he should consult Tieh-so. They decided to hold another public meeting that same day after the midday meal, to explain the activities and organization of the Sacrifice League once more, and call on the villagers to apply for membership.

During the morning Pai-kou came again to ask Little Chang when he would speak, and when he learned of the meeting he took his bowl and walked through the village, broadcasting the news, until the whole village knew of it. When Little Chang had finished his meal, he told the village head he wanted to hold a public meeting that afternoon. The village head agreed, and was just ordering Old Sung to sound the gong when Pai-kou hurried in and said: "Commissioner! Please come to the watch house (the building they had set in order that morning), and make a speech outside."

"I know," said Little Chang. "We were just going to sound the gong to summon everybody."

"No need for the gong," said Pai-kou. "They're all there waiting!"

As he was speaking Little Mao burst in, also to invite Little Chang to go and speak. He picked up the list of names from the table, saying, "Take my list to check off the names!" Little Chang had not yet dealt with the problem of that list, however when Little Mao picked it up he did not stop him.

On reaching the watch house, they found the villagers seated before the gate like the audience in front of a stage waiting for a play to begin. Somebody must have thought of clapping, for when Little Chang arrived two or three began to applaud, some children joined in, and presently the whole group was clapping. A table had been placed above the steps of the watch house, toward which everybody was facing, and Little Chang realized this must be the platform. So he went up, followed by Comrade Wang. And Little Mao climbed up after them, to present his list of names very respectfully to Little Chang.

The clapping stopped and a hush fell as Little Chang unrolled the list of names. Seeing his list being used Little Mao was delighted, whereas Leng-yuan, Tieh-so and their group shook their heads, saying to themselves: "Yesterday evening didn't he say we wouldn't recognize that list? Then why is he using it after all?"

Little Chang simply looked at the last name on the list, and called out: "Tsui Hei-hsiao!"

A man in his thirties stood up and answered, "Present!" He was a famine refugee from Huahsien in Honan, and his clothes looked like so many rags hanging together. He seemed afraid to face people, and after standing up and answering hung his head again.

"Why did you join the league?" Little Chang asked.

"I don't know," answered Tsui with his Honan accent.

"Who introduced you?"

"What?" asked the other, lifting his head. When Little Chang repeated his question, he answered, again with his Honan accent: "I don't understand."

This was the cue for Leng-yuan and his friends.

"Nobody understands!" said one.

"Only Little Mao understands!" said another.

Little Mao lost his temper, and said to Tsui: "Didn't I introduce you?"

"You asked me how old I was," said Tsui, "and wrote down my name. How did I know what you were up to?"

Immediately the jokers chimed in: "Checking on the census!"

"Conscripting soldiers!"

"Practising writing!"...

Little Chang then turned very formally to Little Mao and said: "Comrade! This is not the right way to enrol members! Just think, if they don't even understand the activities and organization of the league, what possible use can they be?"

"He's an outsider," protested Little Mao, "he doesn't understand. I just put down his name at the end, I didn't count him in to begin with."

"Oh," said Little Chang, "so that's how it was? Then let me ask some of the natives!" Unrolling the list again, he called the first name, which was that of Landlord Li. Li answered as best he could, but was unable to give any good reason for joining. Little Chang then questioned others. Some of the more naive answered, "I don't know," while some deliberately gave ridiculous answers, such as "To please the authorities," "In order to get a wife...."

When Little Chang had gone through two pages of names he stopped and turned again very formally to Little Mao, to say, "This won't do! There has not been enough preliminary instruction." Then, addressing the whole group: "I shall not ask any more: apparently no one understands. This league of ours lays great emphasis on voluntary membership. First our propagandists must explain clearly the aims of the league, then anyone who approves those aims must himself find two members to introduce him, and be approved by the local organizer of his district. Only then can he fill up a membership form and become a member. Since this name list is useless, let us start instruction and organization from the beginning again."

"Right!" shouted the youngsters.

"What a pity to have wasted all that paper!" added Leng-yuan.

"Let me first explain our league's activities to you all," continued Little Chang. Then, using the language of the people, he discussed the spirit animating the league's activities, so that every single person in the village understood what the Sacrifice League stood for.

This done, he said: "Now that you all know what the Sacrifice League does, anyone who wants to join in its work is free to register. None of the people on this list joined in the way required by the league. There are only two people in this village who have joined in the proper way: one is Comrade Tieh-so, whom I introduced, the other is Comrade Little Mao, whom Comrade Wang introduced...."

At the mention of Little Mao, there were shouts of: "We don't want Little Mao!"

"We don't want flunkeys!"

Pai-kou, however, pushed his way forward and shouted: "Why don't you want him? The commissioner said, 'People with money contribute money!' He has plenty of money! If we have him, then when the league needs money there won't be any difficulty!"

"The league doesn't need any money!" someone else said. "We don't want him!"

"What do you mean, it doesn't need money?" asked another. "There are lots of ways in which money is needed! Can we fight the Japanese without guns? Let's ask him to buy a few guns for us!"

"Do you think he will buy them?" asked another. "He's fond enough of picking up crumbs from rich people's tables, but to get him to fork out is another matter."

"He'll have no choice," said Leng-yuan. "Didn't you hear what the commissioner said: 'Members must obey the rules of the league'? 'People with money contribute money' is a rule so long as he is a member!"

When he heard that he would have to contribute money, Little Mao began to regret having joined, but he saw no way of backing out. However, while he was wavering someone else said: "Even if he contributes money we don't want him."

He therefore seized this opportunity to say: "If you really don't want me, I'll drop out." And to Little Chang: "Commissioner! Can someone who has joined the league leave it?"

"According to our rules," said Little Chang, "you are free to join or resign as you please. But it's better not to leave if you don't have to, because the more members we have, the stronger we are."

"No!" said Little Mao in a low voice. "They are all opposed to me, and you don't want to spoil the spirit of the league just on my account!" He fondly imagined Little Chang did not know what sort of person he really was, and that he could use unselfishness in the public interest as a pretext for withdrawing, as if he were sacrificing himself for the common good. Little Chang realized he was only resigning because he was afraid of contributing money, but he did not press the matter, and answered very politely in a low voice: "As you think best! Entirely as you feel!"

Upon obtaining permission to resign, Little Mao not only felt no shame, but immediately announced: "No need for you to say any more. I have already received the commissioner's permission to resign!" The whole group thereupon started clapping and roaring with laughter.

Not wanting Little Mao to lose face, Little Chang had not intended to announce this publicly, but now he stated: "Although Comrade Little Mao has decided to resign, later we shall still ask him to help us outside the league! This means the only member left in the village is Tieh-so. From this evening onward, Comrade Wang and I shall be staying in this building, and anyone who wants to join the league can come here to register. Comrade Wang, Tieh-so and I can all three act as sponsors. I have other villages to go to, but Comrade Wang can stay a little longer to help you set up your village branch of the league." After this the meeting was adjourned.

That evening Leng-yuan, Pai-kou and a few other enthusiasts made a tour of the village, and over thirty people applied for membership. Seeing how well things were going, Little Chang did not leave the next day, but held an inaugural meeting then and there to elect officers. Tieh-so was elected secretary, Old Yang organizer, and Leng-yuan propagandist. After the election of officers Little Chang and Comrade Wang explained to the league members how to divide into small groups and elect group leaders, and they decided on the procedure for future meetings. Thus this branch was established.

9

THE EVENING OF THE DAY THAT THE INAUGURAL MEET-
ing of the village branch of the Sacrifice League
was held, Little Chang and Comrade Wang were
talking with Tieh-so and a few other young enthusiasts when a middle-aged man in a long gown
came in and handed a visiting card to Little Chang,
saying: "Commissioner! My father invites you and
Comrade Wang to come over to our shop for a chat!"

Little Chang took the card and read the name
"Wang." "Who is this?" he asked Tieh-so. "How
is it you haven't mentioned him to me?"

"He's the manager of our village grocery shop,"
said Leng-yuan. "When he was young he went to
Tientsin, he's a very enlightened old fellow. Ever
since we heard of the Japanese aggression, whenever
anyone comes from the county or the district, he
always asks how the fighting is going."

119

"Do go!" others urged. "If you give the old chap some news of victories he will be very pleased, and he will spread the good news!"

"Very well," said Little Chang. So he and Comrade Wang went with Wang's son to the grocery shop.

An old man with a grey beard and high nose came out of the shop to welcome them, ceremoniously taking off his glasses to nod to them. Then, putting his glasses on again, he asked them to come into the office. A tray had been set ready on the table in the office with a pot of wine and several dishes—common things like eggs and beancurd, but fresh and clean. The sight of these preparations made Little Chang suspect they were going to be asked a favour—some gentry in the town, wanting to evade legitimate taxes, had previously staged several such scenes. However, having come he had to sit down. If Wang made any unreasonable request he could still refuse, as he had done in the town, even after drinking his wine and eating his food.

This time, however, Little Chang's guess was wrong. Old Wang, unlike the town gentry, had no ulterior motive and had never entertained other people who came from the district. His friendliness was genuine, for he had a special respect for him. Within two or three months of the outbreak of war the Japanese had, to his amazement, broken through Yenmenkuan, a pass in Shansi. Every time he heard of a Japanese advance he would ruffle his grey hair in agitation and stutter: "Wh-wh-where have all our Chinese troops got to?"

He had no idea how the war was fought. He asked the village head who had received training, but the village head could not give him a satisfactory reply. Visitors from the county and district could sometimes give him news of defeat, but sometimes they knew even less than he, and were quite unable to explain events. And though men came to organize corps or societies, they all had the same outlook as Hsiao-hsi and Chun-hsi, and did nothing but compile a few worthless lists of names. Wang did not know what the outcome would be if things went on like this. Then he heard that Little Chang had come, and felt here was a chance to ask for details. He too had only heard of Little Chang after Tieh-so's arrest. That was when Communists were being suppressed, so he did not dare express approval openly; however, secretly he did so, because he had long felt that unless those rogues and bullies were overthrown, the world would not be fit to live in.

But when he heard Little Chang was a Communist, he was rather taken aback. He did not believe what Chun-hsi and the rest said about Communists killing people and burning property. His impression of the Communists was derived from their name: he felt that once the Communists came that would be the end of private ownership and everything would become common property. "In that case," he thought, "everybody will want to sit at table and eat: who will do productive work?" So when he heard that Little Chang was a Communist he said to himself: "Such a good person, it's a pity he's a Communist."

Leaning on his stick, he, like everybody else, had groped through the dark to Tieh-so's doorway to hear Little Chang speak, and the next noon he had arrived at the watch house very early for the meeting, and drunk in everything that was said. These two speeches convinced him that Little Chang's reputation was well deserved: he knew what he was talking about, had foresight, looked beneath the surface of things, and spoke well. Old Wang listened specially to hear what he would say about Communism, but neither time did Little Chang mention it. Now his reason for inviting Little Chang, apart from questioning him as to the outcome of the war, was to ask him if he really were a Communist.

Old Wang drank with Little Chang and Comrade Wang. Then his assistant brought in the rice. Having already had their meal, they ate very little of the dishes. When they had finished eating and drinking, Wang started asking questions about the military situation. Little Chang realized that the old man really took the affairs of the country to heart, so he first gave a very comprehensive account of the enemy's movements during recent months and the military situation on all fronts, and then explained what Chairman Mao Tse-tung of the Chinese Communist Party had told reporters about the idea of a protracted war. (At that time the book "On Protracted War" had not yet been published.) Old Wang had seen great cities and was eager to get a general picture of the situation. Unfortunately other men from the county and district could only give him isolated scraps of news, so that the more he heard the more impatient he became. Now, however, as he listened to Little Chang he got a very clear picture of the situation, and there was no need for him to interrupt with questions. In the pauses between the narrative he would make a circling movement with his head, as if waking· up from a dream, and say, "Ah... so!"

When Little Chang had finished he remained silent for some time, and then said frowning: "In this case, it will be a long business, won't it?"

His conception of the war was very simple. He thought that if the Japanese came, the best thing was to stop them. If they could not stop the enemy, then retreat. During their retreat if they had the opportunity they should attack again, but failing that they should hold what territory they had. And when they could hold that territory no longer they should retreat again. If they were finally driven into a corner and could not hold out, then probably that would be the end. Now Little Chang had said that this village might be lost, yet even if it were lost and there were Japanese all around, both within this circle and outside it they could still resist. They would have to fight the Japanese many times, until finally they defeated them. Such a possibility had never occurred to him before. He did not like the prospect of such hard times ahead, so frowning even more deeply after Little Chang finished speaking he said: "In this case, it will be a long business, won't it?"

"Don't you agree?" countered Little Chang.

"Oh yes, I do," said Old Wang. "You have grounds for all you say. Since such is the case, how can I think otherwise? Only I feel this really is a hard business. But then if we don't put up with it what else can we do? Anyway, in the end we will be able to beat the Japanese, and it's worth putting up with a little hardship for that." Then tugging at his grey beard again he said: "I'm already sixty, it doesn't matter whether I see the end of this business or not, all I want is for the younger ones to escape falling into the hands of the Japanese! All these months since the war started I have been feeling at a loss, but now at last I feel I understand what it is all about."

"Mr. Chang!" he went on. "Let me ask you something else! Is the Sacrifice League Communist?"

Little Chang thought the question rather a strange one, but since it had been asked, he had to answer. "Of course not!" he said. "The Sacrifice League is an organization for resisting Japan and saving the country. The Communist Party is a political party. The two organizations are quite different."

"They tell me, sir, that you are a Communist," said Old Wang. "How is it that you have become a commissioner of the Sacrifice League?"

"There's nothing strange about that," said Little Chang. "Any one who's willing to sacrifice himself to save the country, no matter whether he belongs to any party or not, can join the Sacrifice League."

"I understand that," said Wang. "But I have a word of advice for you, sir, if you'll excuse my presumption."

Little Chang supposed the old man had discovered some fault in him, and immediately assured him: "Of course, that's good! We are very glad to hear people's criticism."

"Excuse my frankness," said Wang, "but why should such a good and talented gentleman as yourself have joined the Communists? I can't help thinking that a flaw in your character."

Greatly surprised, Little Chang said, laughing: "Manager Wang, I'm sure you've never met a Communist before, have you?"

"No," said Old Wang. "Only I feel Communism is no good. If everybody starts eating what is available, who will do productive work?"

Realizing what his view of Communism was, Little Chang had to explain it to him. He talked for some time on the meaning of Socialism and Communism, and finally told him Communism did not mean sharing these few acres of land or these few houses; but only when manual labour had been largely replaced by machines could Communism be realized. It was the final social system the Communists wished to establish. And he told him what the socialist Soviet Union was like. Little Chang talked for a long time before he could destroy the impression of Communism Old Wang had built up in his own mind.

Wang thought for a time, then said, "I was thinking a gentleman like you ought not to have any foolishness left. It seems I am the one who is foolish. I thought Communism was just breaking up and doing away with personal property. According to you, a worker in the Soviet Union is much more comfortable than a shop-manager like me.

"But to build up a society like that is not going to be easy," he went on, after another pause for thought. "I shan't live to see it, so let's talk of things in the immediate future: the Japanese will soon be here, and the most important thing of course is to save the country. I'm Chinese too, I ought to do what I can. But I like to do practical things. In the past some people came with propaganda about saving the country, but no matter how well they spoke I felt they were wrong and paid no attention to them, knowing it only amounted to so much empty talk. But now you have come, and you are different from the rest of them: when I listen to you I don't feel you say a single word that isn't practical. If you don't think an old fellow like me too useless, I would like to join your Sacrifice League and do what I can. I can't accomplish much, but I can do my bit. That is, of course, if you're willing."

"Of course you are welcome!" exclaimed Little Chang and Comrade Wang together.

"It's very difficult to find enthusiastic old gentlemen like you!" added Little Chang.

Their friendliness made Old Wang take heart, and he stood up, saying, "I believe in doing practical things, and though I'm not really rich, still I'm not like those landlords who are frightened away as soon as contributing money is mentioned. When the league really needs money I'll contribute as much as I can! I don't mind bankrupting this small shop of mine to raise money! Apparently the Japanese devils will soon be here to make trouble, and what use will these few things be then? When the eyes are nearly gone what good are a few eyelashes?"

When Little Chang and Comrade Wang heard this, they admired him all the more, and both praised him. Little Chang said there was no immediate necessity for raising funds, the first important task was to reduce taxes and interest, and arouse the masses to resist Japan. For if they could inspire the majority of the people with the spirit to resist Japan, and then organize them, they could carry on a protracted war against the enemy. They asked him if he had leased land or loaned money for interest, and if so, whether he would set an example for others.

"That's easy!" said Wang. "Only I'm a merchant, I have no land to rent out. The money loaned out is not much either, it only amounts to about four or five thousand, reckoning in terms of silver dollars. I'm afraid it won't be much use as an example!"

"The force of an example doesn't depend on the amount involved," said Little Chang, "and in any case four or five thousand silver dollars is by no means a small sum. At least it will influence one district!"

"I can do that at once," said Wang. "Presently I'll tell the accountant to go through the books, and in the twelfth month when we settle accounts I can put it into practice! I won't just reduce one fifth according to law: there are some accounts on which I've collected interest for several years, and I can let even the principal go!"

Now that they saw eye to eye, they talked till late at night. As they were leaving, Little Chang grasped Wang's hand and said, "Old Comrade, from now on we shall look on you as one of our own people! Whenever you come to town you must stay in our league hostel."

"Whenever you are in this neighbourhood," said Old Wang, "you must be sure to come here!" And so they took their leave.

The fact that sixty-year-old Wang had joined the Sacrifice League and was voluntarily cutting his rate of interest was reported in the official bulletin when Little Chang went back to the county seat. In the village it was proclaimed by Tieh-so and others in the Sacrifice League, while Old Wang spoke of it himself to all he met. Thus in a few days peasants of Li Village and from outside, who had rented land or borrowed money, knew that the government had ordered that rents and rates of interest be reduced, and—what was more—that there were already people putting this into practice. Many peasants therefore asked their own landlords and creditors for a reduction. The Sacrifice Leagues in the various villages helped, and very soon this had grown into a movement.

Landlord Li lived on his rents and the interest on money loaned. Hsiao-hsi and Chun-hsi too had been small-scale usurers ever since they came back in 1930 with their pockets well-lined. And even Little Mao privately lent out small sums. Now they heard discussions everywhere on reducing rents and interest, while Old Wang of their own village had not only voluntarily reduced his rate of interest but was always encouraging other people to do the same, and the majority of their tenants and debtors, having joined the Sacrifice League, were constantly attending meetings in the watch house and uniting to demand a reduction. The situation was serious and they must take immediate steps to remedy it. Li told Chun-hsi to go to the county seat and call on the captain of the county Righteous Brigade. Chun-hsi spent one day in town, and came home the next day to tell Li the result of his trip.

That evening Li sent for Hsiao-hsi and Little Mao, and they gathered by his opium lamp to hear Chun-hsi's report. It was a quiet night and the front gate was locked as Chun-hsi took out a slip of paper on which he had jotted notes, and told them: "I went to the county brigade headquarters and presented the problems Uncle raised to the county brigade captain. The captain was very pleased by our marked concern for the overall situation, so he went to the trouble of giving a detailed answer to each of the points raised. He said the most important thing is resisting the Communists. This Righteous Brigade of ours was originally set up for this purpose, and now there has been no real change, except that our methods must be more subtle. There is no contradiction between resisting the Communists and making use of them. Commander Yen has said, 'I want only filial sons, not patriots!'—meaning that he will use anyone who works for him. The same applies naturally to the Communists: we must make use of them without allowing them to make use of us. Although there has been an alliance with the Communists our Righteous Brigade has been kept, in the first place to utilise them to work for us, in the second place to watch carefully to see if they are really working for Commander Yen. If we see any Communist still working for the Communist Party and not for Commander Yen, we should report it secretly, and Commander Yen can remove him from his post.

"The second problem was, 'Is the Sacrifice League Communist?' He says many of the officers of the Sacrifice League are Communists, because they are able to organize young people, and Commander Yen is making use of them for this. Of course some of them want to make use of the Sacrifice League to spread Communism, but Commander Yen is not afraid of that. As president of the Sacrifice League, he can use his authority to punish such people."

"Then didn't he say how we could deal with the Sacrifice League?" put in Landlord Li.

"He did," said Chun-hsi. "He said the best thing would be to get the leadership of the village Sacrifice League into our own hands. Failing that, then use all means to discredit the league, until finally it loses its effectiveness."

"What did I say?" Li glared at Little Mao. "We had already got it in our hands, but as soon as they mentioned 'cash contributions' you were frightened away! Actually, once you had control of it, you needn't have given money unless you felt like it; but once you let it go they got hold of it, and now they want even more money from you! Aren't they trying to force us now to observe the law about reducing rents and interest?" He turned to Chun-hsi. "Why did Commander Yen make that law about reducing rents and interest?"

"I'm just coming to that," said Chun-hsi. "The county captain said this reduction of rents and interest was originally proposed by the Communists. They requested Commander Yen to make it a law, and because Commander Yen wanted them to believe he is revolutionary, he agreed. But this is just eyewash. It all depends on how things are done. If the power is in our hands, we can choose those people who can't pay the rent or interest anyway, and let some of them off. Then we make a statement announcing this, to get ourselves a good name while actually not losing anything. But if the power is in their hands they will organize the tenants and debtors to settle accounts with us, so that we will actually lose money, at the same time getting a bad name for only reducing under compulsion."

Li glared at Little Mao again, and the latter said remorsefully: "After all they showed foresight. What a pity I didn't think of this at the time."

"As soon as they mentioned money you were terrified!" said Hsiao-hsi with a chuckle. "How could you think of anything else?" Then they all burst out laughing.

"When I had finished asking about these problems," continued Chun-hsi, "I reported what had happened since Little Chang came to the village to set up a Sacrifice League. He said many places were sending in similar reports: apparently Little Chang is using the Sacrifice League to spread Communism. He is notifying all areas to collect such material, and when there is enough evidence he will go to Commander Yen. As long as there is material, there is no difficulty about getting him transferred. This was all I talked about with the county captain this time."

"Now that we have heard your report, we must make our plans accordingly," said Hsiao-hsi. "There are two things to be done at once: the first is to find a way to obstruct this reduction of rents and interest, the second is to find a way to make this Sacrifice League with Tieh-so and the others lose its effectiveness."

"To obstruct the reduction of rents and interest," put in Little Mao, "I think the county captain's plan is a good one—that is for us to let off those people who can't pay anyway."

"I don't think that will do," said Li. "Since that's what the county captain said, it's obvious that method has already been used. One strategy can only be used once or twice: if everybody uses it people will see through it. I think although we have Tieh-so and the rest with their Sacrifice League in the village, the real power is still in our hands: the village head is one of us, and Chun-hsi is captain of the Righteous Brigade. If we hold a general mobilization meeting, of the three bodies represented—the Righteous Brigade, the Sacrifice League and the village government—two are ours. So we can still manage things as we like."

"That gives me an idea," said Chun-hsi. "We can find a way to delay matters. When the general mobilization meeting is held, let's raise this question ourselves. We'll discuss it with the village head, telling him we want to organize an Investigation Committee for the Reduction of Rents and Interest to make an investigation of the whole village, prior to reducing rents and interest systematically. Since Tieh-so and the others can't write, we can prepare a very detailed and elaborate form to be filled in slowly; and when all the forms are filled, we can say it has to be reported to the authorities. By marking time like this we can delay half a year."

"But after half a year won't we still have to reduce?" interrupted Little Mao.

"I think in less than two months the Japanese will be here," said Hsiao-hsi, "so what are you afraid of? And this is only a suggestion, it only means stopping the Sacrifice League from talking. If we can think of a way to discredit the league and make it useless, this business will be shelved and no one will follow it up."

"Right!" said Li. "If only the Sacrifice League were disbanded, no one would trouble about these things which aren't their business. Let's think first how to get the Sacrifice League disbanded."

"I've an idea," said Hsiao-hsi. "I may not be able to achieve good deeds, but I'm a skilled mischiefmaker. I can upset this little apple-cart of theirs."

"Don't blow your own trumpet!" said Chun-hsi. "Tell us your idea and we'll see whether it's any good or not. Times have changed, and we can't have it all our own way. Since that fellow Chang came here he seems to have emboldened Tieh-so and those other clodhoppers. Your old high-handed ways probably won't work any more."

"It only means we have to watch for a favourable opportunity," said Hsiao-hsi. "Do you suppose I don't realize that? Being high-handed doesn't matter: as long as it's cleverly done we shall succeed!"

"There you go, boasting again," said Chun-hsi. "Keep to the point! What's your idea?"

"This is my idea," said Hsiao-hsi, "and I guarantee you will think it a clever one! Aren't Tieh-so and his group all young men? Aren't I the captain of the Self Defence Corps? I shall say the situation now is critical, so the authorities have sent orders for us to intensify our training. In the morning I will summon them to parade, in the evening I shall make them sleep together, ready to go into action at a moment's notice, keeping them on the move from morning to night so that they have no time to hold meetings. Then they can't get up to any tricks, the authorities will praise my sense of duty, and nobody can say anything against me!"

Without waiting for Chun-hsi to speak, Li gave a guffaw, and exclaimed: "Good for you, Hsiao-hsi my boy!" Both Chun-hsi and Little Mao praised him too.

Having laid their plot, the four of them were in the best of spirits. Li was in such a good humour that, contrary to his custom, he let them use his Yihsing pottery pipe and Taiku opium lamp to have a good smoke.

Sure enough, Tieh-so and his group proved powerless to defeat the others' cunning scheme. There was a general mobilization meeting in the village which passed the investigation of rents and interest and training of the Self Defence Corps. After the Self Defence Corps started going into training, all the young, able-bodied men in the village were busy from morning to night, and had no time for anything else. Although Comrade Wang paid several visits to the village, unfortunately he was young and could not see through these ruses. He saw only that the forms were very comprehensive and the training very thorough, and thinking the rogues were working conscientiously for the public good he praised them highly.

Old Wang, however, did not approve. It was not that he saw through their scheme, but he was a practical man and realized such methods were not getting anywhere, hence his disapproval. One day he went into town again, and when Little Chang asked him about the work in the village, with many shakes of the head he told him, "No matter how good the cause, once Hsiao-hsi, Chun-hsi and their group are involved, nothing good can come of it, not if you wait a thousand years. Take the case of reducing rents and interest. My way was to make an announcement myself and then reduce them, but they won't do anything so practical, they must first bring the matter up at a general mobilization meeting and slowly fill up investigation forms. It seems to me before they have completed the forms the Japanese will already be here. Since you left, the Sacrifice League has not held a single meeting. That Hsiao-hsi wants to train the Self Defence Corps, so in the daytime he makes them run in circles and march, in the evening he assembles them to sleep in the temple. The result is the young people in the village can't even sleep when they want to, and have no time at all for anything else. As I see it, it's not the slightest use! No matter how round the circles they run, or how quietly they march, what good is it?"

Little Chang was very experienced. From what Wang said he knew someone was up to mischief, and when he questioned the county Self Defence Corps captain, the latter said: "Who told Hsiao-hsi to train like that?" The county captain sent someone to take over Hsiao-hsi's post, transferring him to the town for training.

In this way Hsiao-hsi's scheme was thwarted. But just at that time Commander Yen decided his Dare-to-Die troops were learning too much from the Eighth Route Army, and would prove hard to control, so he sent old army officers out in all directions to enlist new troops. These troops were also called "guerilla troops." The officer sent to their county was an old company commander named Tien, and Hsiao-hsi, unwilling to go into town for training, joined Tien's detachment.

10

THE NEW SELF DEFENCE CORPS CAPTAIN SENT BY
the county authorities was also a member of the
Sacrifice League, so when he came to the village,
far from preventing the league from holding meetings,
he took part himself. And every evening he would
talk with the members. If there were any business
they talked business, otherwise they discussed guerilla
tactics; and while he did not obstruct the work of the
league, he greatly improved the training of the Self
Defence Corps. The work of the Sacrifice League
began to go more smoothly, and since Old Wang had
already reduced his rate of interest the villagers
requested Landlord Li to follow suit, instead of just
filling up forms while actually doing nothing. Li had
nothing to say for himself, and could only hope that
the enemy would hurry up and arrive, so that he could
gain time.

Sure enough, in a few days the news became more disquieting, for the Peking-Hankow and Cheng-ting-Taiyuan railways were taken by the enemy. The Sacrifice League concentrated on urging everybody to move away foodstuffs, and shelved the question of reducing rents and interest. Li did not benefit from this, however, because from the Peking-Hankow and Chengting-Taiyuan railways retreated the Fifty-third Army, the Ninety-first Division, the Fourth Cavalry Division, the Hopei-Chahar Guerilla Army and the so-called First Army of the World. . . . All these troops retreated to Shansi to the Shangtang area. Most Kuomintang troops were in the habit of firing their rifles as soon as they entered a village, and once they had frightened away the country people they proceeded to loot. They demanded food from all whom they met, and those who could give them nothing they beat. The village head trained under Yen Hsi-shan made off secretly, and the district head fled too. Li's usual cunning was quite lost on these veteran soldiers, and finally he was kidnapped and held for ransom by the Hou Brigade under Sun.

When Li's family wanted to ransom him, they could find no one to negotiate the price. The decent villagers were only sorry he was not dead, and would not lift a finger to help him, while the rogues were all afraid. Chun-hsi dared not go, Little Mao was even more terrified, and as for the other opium addicts and gamblers, although usually only too glad to have a smoke with him, now that this had happened they took care to keep out of sight. After a long consultation between Li's family, Chun-hsi and Little

Mao, all agreed that the only man for the job was Hsiao-hsi. So they sent a messenger to the Tien Detachment to fetch him back. Hsiao-hsi was looking for just such opportunities and went willingly to find the Hou Brigade. He was away for three days, by which time Li's family, having heard nothing, was beginning to be worried. On the fourth day Little Mao and Chun-hsi were at Li's house as usual, discussing how to make further inquiries, when at midday Li and Hsiao-hsi arrived.

Asked how they had come back, Hsiao-hsi replied complacently: "As soon as I got there they sent a staff officer to negotiate with me.

" 'Our troops' conditions are very hard,' he said. 'We brought your uncle here simply to ask him for some National Salvation contributions.'

" 'That's easy,' I said. 'I guarantee I can think of a means to help get something for the troops. Although my uncle has a little land, he has no ready money; and in times like these nobody wants to buy land, so don't expect anything from him.'

"When the staff officer saw I understood the business myself, he insisted on lighting the opium lamp and inviting me to have a good smoke, and the two of us talked frankly for some time. He said I must help them to get some things before they would let Uncle go, and I agreed. After two or three days, operating in the night too, I helped them to get several dozen donkey-loads of cloth, oil and wine. They were very pleased, and entertained me and Uncle to several good meals before sending us back."

When Li's family learned that he had not spent a cent, of course they were overjoyed; and Chun-hsi and Little Mao admired Hsiao-hsi's ability. Little Mao wanted to know where he had managed to get several dozen loads of things. "No need to ask!" said Hsiao-hsi. "It was just going begging!"

It was New Year by the lunar calendar, but because of the unsettled times nobody had the heart to celebrate New Year, and scarcely anybody had so much as steamed a dumpling. Relatives did not exchange presents, and instead of wishing each other a happy New Year, their first words on meeting were:

"Which troops are staying in your village?"

"Have they stolen much?"

They had to put up with this till the Lantern Festival[1] when Japanese planes came to bomb the county seat, and a few days later the enemy fought their way from Changchih. Although Li Village was only four or five miles from the highway, the main enemy force passed it by, only some mounted scouts coming through every few days to reconnoitre. The little bands of Kuomintang troops who had shown themselves so fierce when robbing the people no sooner heard the sound of guns than they fled to the mountains, leaving only a few disbanded soldiers who started looting even more savagely than before.

The village Self Defence Corps had never fought, and their only weapons were one rifle and two hand grenades. Unable to put up any resistance, they simply kept watch outside the village, and when the

---

[1] The fifteenth of the first month by the lunar calendar.

enemy or bandits were seen approaching they would send word to the village so that everybody could hide.

Landlord Li had already had one fright, so whenever he heard there was anything afoot he would scuttle into his underground shelter. And Chun-hsi, who had no shelter of his own, always took refuge with Li.

One day, toward sunset, Little Mao rushed in to tell Li and Chun-hsi: "That Comrade Wang has come back. They say he is the head of our district."

"What good is a district head?" said Li. "Look at all the troops that fled!"

They had only spoken a few words when they heard people outside saying: "About a dozen disbanded soldiers have come." In alarm Li, Chun-hsi and Little Mao barred the front gate and hid in the shelter. After a while, all being still, Li sent Little Mao to look through a crack in the window upstairs. When Little Mao got up there he saw a soldier heading straight toward their front gate. Thoroughly frightened, he was about to go and report it to Li, when he saw it was Hsiao-hsi. So he called out to him softly.

Hsiao-hsi recognized Little Mao's voice, and answered, "So it's you! Open up quickly!"

"I hear there are over a dozen disbanded soldiers about," said Little Mao.

"That's all right," said Hsiao-hsi. "Never you mind. Just open up." Little Mao opened the door and let him in, and then went to the shelter to fetch Li and Chun-hsi out.

"Hsiao-hsi! Who did you come with?" asked Li. "Where is the Tien Detachment stationed?"

"I spent several days at the headquarters of the Hou Brigade," said Hsiao-hsi. "Then the Japanese came, and I don't know where the Tien Detachment has got to. The Hou Brigade has gone into the mountains at Lingchuan, but I stayed in the neighbourhood. Then I met someone I knew, a man called Wang from northern Honan whom I met before in Taiyuan." Then turning to Chun-hsi: "Maybe you know the man: in 1930 when Commander Yen decided to set up a Forty-eighth Division there was a group of people who wanted to join. He stayed in Taiyuan for a few days. I was adjutant in the Forty-eighth Division Headquarters and talked to him several times. Then Commander Yen was beaten so it didn't come off. This time they came over here with Sun's guerillas. A few days ago Sun's troops went to the east mountain and Wang got hold of several dozen men to stay in White Dragon Temple, then gathered some more disbanded soldiers. He calls himself Commander Wang. I'm his chief of staff, and we operate in that neighbourhood."

"The last few days I've been at a loose end at home, not daring to go out," said Li. "What is the situation here? You tell me about it."

"The main facts are these," said Hsiao-hsi. "The Japanese are in control of the highway and the county seat. There's a committee in town, headed by a man called Wei." Then turning again to Chun-hsi: "Maybe you know the man. He is a fat fellow, in Taiyuan he was always going to Fifth Master's house, and later he became purchasing agent of the Opium Prohibition Inspection Office."

"I know him!" said Chun-hsi.

"He's responsible for maintaining order in the city," went on Hsiao-hsi. Outside the city there is a Japanese garrison every few miles along the road, sometimes as many as one or two squads, sometimes as few as three or four men. And mounted troops are constantly patrolling up and down, occasionally going into the neighbouring villages. All the villages by the main road have their own committees, and the Japanese troops call on them when they pass."

"What connection have you made with the Japanese troops and the town committee?" asked Li.

"I've no connection as yet," replied Hsiao-hsi. "White Dragon Temple is in the mountain, nearly ten miles from the highway: we don't go onto the highway, and they don't go into the mountain, so we never meet!"

"It's really no joke living at home," said Li. "Every day endless deserters keep coming...."

"Deserters don't matter," said Hsiao-hsi. "The other troops have all gone: for about ten miles around there are only isolated groups of five or ten soldiers— they're all our lot. When you see them you have only to say you know me, and I guarantee you will have no trouble."

"Although you say so," said Li, "still one feels uneasy. If there's good order in town, it would be better to move into town to live. Could you write me a letter of introduction to that Mr. Wei?"

"If it's him, I know him," put in Chun-hsi. "I can go and make enquiries for you, Uncle, and if everything is all right, I'll go with you. Perhaps I'll be able to find some kind of job!"

Just then shouting was heard outside. Little Mao went to the door to listen, and came back saying: "The people on the road say they have caught ten deserters and captured six rifles."

Hsiao-hsi jumped up and said: "Who caught them?"

"They say it was the Self Defence Corps."

"Damnation!" said Hsiao-hsi. "I must be going!" So saying he started out, feeling for the pistol in his belt.

Little Mao followed, asking, "What's up?" Hsiao-hsi paid no attention, just waving him back, then opened the door and went out. Li looked at Chun-hsi and Chun-hsi looked at Li. Little Mao hurried over to ask what it meant, but they could not make head or tail of it. They remained silent for some time until they heard the sound of tramping feet drawing nearer and nearer. Little Mao jumped up to close the gate, but it was already too late. Meantime Li and Chun-hsi, thinking bandits had come, hastily took refuge in the shelter. They were not bandits who came in but Comrade Wang and the captain of the Self Defence Corps, at the head of about twenty Self Defence guards who looked very militant with the newly captured rifles on their backs. Leng-yuan was in front, carrying a rifle. As soon as he came into the courtyard he grabbed Little Mao and asked: "Did Hsiao-hsi come here?"

Little Mao was too frightened to speak and could only stutter, "N-n-no."

A good many of the villagers were crowding in behind, and one said, "He did come! I met him!"

144

Leng-yuan pointed his rifle at Little Mao and said: "Tell the truth! Did he come?"

Little Mao, bent almost double, answered: "He did come, but he left again."

"Make a search," said Comrade Wang. "Don't let him slip through our fingers!" Everybody began searching Li's house. When they reached the shelter they found Li and Chun-hsi, but no Hsiao-hsi; and when they questioned them they gave the same answer as Little Mao, so they knew he had escaped and let it go at that.

A big group comprising the captain of the Self Defence Corps, Comrade Wang, the Self Defence guards and some of the villagers, went back to the watch house. The watch house was being guarded by two guards with rifles, who had locked the ten captured deserters inside.

"How shall we deal with these ten men?" Leng-yuan asked Comrade Wang, pointing to the watch house door.

"I think since there are so many people here, we had better first call a meeting," said Wang, "and deal with them after the meeting. Some of you go from house to house to summon everybody. The best thing would be for the whole village to attend."

By now the enemy was not far away, so it was not convenient to sound the gong for a meeting. Leng-yuan, Tieh-so and a few other enthusiasts ran from house to house announcing the meeting; and since deserters had just been captured, and everybody wanted to have a look at them, more villagers turned up than usual. Soon everybody had assembled. The village head had run away a fortnight earlier, while, because Hsiao-hsi was involved, Li and Chun-hsi who were deputy head and captain of the Righteous Brigade dared not appear. When Tieh-so saw that there was no one from the village administration office he realized that as village secretary of the Sacrifice League, he should preside over the meeting. Accordingly he mounted the steps of the watch house and said: "Comrade Wang has now become head of our district. Today he has come to our village to work, and wants first to hold a meeting with you all. So now I'll ask Comrade Wang to speak."

"Countrymen! Comrades!" said Comrade Wang. "The Japanese are already here, our county seat and main highways are already in enemy hands. Now, as Commissioner Chang told you last time he was here, we are in a position to resist behind the enemy's lines. Although the enemy has taken our towns and chief highways, still the wide countryside is in our hands. In future we must make use of the open country to carry on a protracted war with the enemy, fighting and holding out, sticking it out and fighting until the enemy is worn out and we can recover our lost territory. Don't lose heart because you have seen so many Chinese troops retreating. I'm going to give you some good news. You all know the Eighth Route Army and the great fight at Pinghsingkuan in Shansi Province? Now although other armies are retreating southward the Eighth Route Army is advancing northward, and has retaken Ningwu, Kuangling, Lingchiu, Tanghsien, Fanchih, Tsoyun, Yiuyu, Ningtsin and Sohsien.... At all these places in the enemy's rear, the Eighth Route Army will set up centres of anti-Japanese resistance to carry out a protracted war.

"Now the army has come from Hungtung and Chaohsien to our district, and wants in collaboration with us countryfolk to set up a centre to resist the enemy. Unfortunately the old administrators were a poor lot. In ordinary times it was all very well for them to stand on their dignity to impress the people, but in this present emergency they are useless. A fortnight ago when the news became serious, all the armies retreated, the county magistrate fell ill of fright and the district and village heads ran away, leaving just the common people to be trampled on by the enemy and exposed to the brutality of disbanded soldiers, with no one in charge. When I wired Commander Yen's headquarters, he had just retreated from Linfen and was unable even to look after himself, while all his 'filial' subordinates were hurrying after him, only afraid to be left behind. Nobody was willing to take office here. Finally a member of our Sacrifice League was elected county magistrate, but he had only been in office three days when the enemy arrived. After the county government moved out of the city there was no order at all, and not a single district or village head, so through our Commissioner Chang some members of the Sacrifice League were chosen to act as district heads. And I'm the head of this district.

"This district of ours is just like all the others: the village heads who received the 'filial' training have all fled to the last man. Now I am coming to each village to do two things: to select anti-Japanese cadres, and

147

to organize work here. In this village no national salvation society of any kind has been set up, and that will have to wait till later. The most important village office is that of village head, so you had better elect a head at once. Elect someone now!"

Some people proposed Old Wang, some Old Yang.

Then Leng-yuan jumped up and said: "My idea is this: things are in such a state, the village head will not only have to be a keen worker, he must also be young and active and able to move about quickly. I propose Tieh-so!"

Without waiting for the chairman to ask for a vote, everybody shouted "Right!" Then District Head Wang asked them to show hands, and again the whole group voted for Tieh-so as village head. Although Li was deputy head, since he had protected Hsiao-hsi the villagers said he could not remain in office, and they elected Old Wang. As for the captain of the Self Defence Corps, all said he was excellent and must on no account be changed. When officers had been elected they discussed a scheme of work. However, this village was so close to the enemy that apart from making everybody swear not to become traitors other anti-Japanese resistance or curfew work had to be left to the officers to consider. When District Head Wang had concluded, everybody asked him to describe how the ten deserters had been captured, and to try them. Thereupon District Head Wang asked the captain of the Self Defence Corps to make a report.

"We had just finished our midday meal today when District Head Wang arrived," said the captain. "He called all the members of the Sacrifice League to a meeting in the grocery shop, while the Self Defence Corps kept watch outside the village. Late in the afternoon a guard reported that about ten disbanded soldiers were coming down the mountain path west of the village, and were digging up the things buried by Old Wang in the caves there. So I took several guards to go and look. We saw from a distance that there was only one sentry, and Leng-yuan said this cave had only one entrance, so if we could just capture that sentry we could shut the others up inside. He went to investigate. He crept up the slope behind the sentry, then leapt boldly down, grabbing him from behind and pushing him over, while other guards seized his rifle. Although the sentry called out once, the others in the cave didn't hear. Then taking our two hand grenades I went to the mouth of the cave and threw down one of them. When it exploded some-one thrust his head out, but ducked back at once in fright. I gripped the pin of the other hand grenade and said: 'Get back! Whoever moves will be blown to pieces!' When they were all quiet, I ordered them: 'Pile your rifles up at the entrance! If you don't surrender your rifles I'll blow up the cave and bury you all inside!'

"They didn't say anything, and after a moment a man came out and placed five rifles at the door. I thought they had more, and said: 'Why don't you surrender them all?'

"One of them said, 'We only have six rifles, the sentry took one.'

"The guard who had been on sentry duty outside the village confirmed that they only had six rifles, so that was all right. Leng-yuan went down and collected the rifles, and then we ordered them to come out. I asked them what regiment they were in, and they said they didn't belong to any regiment, but had been called together at the last moment by Company Commander Wang in the Hou Brigade. They live in White Dragon Temple and Hsiao-hsi is their chief of staff. It was Hsiao-hsi who brought them here to dig up the cave. Hsiao-hsi was afraid the villagers might recognize him, so after pointing out the cave to them he had hidden himself. That's how these ten men were caught."

The members of the Self Defence Corps and the Sacrifice League already knew this, but the later arrivals did not, and after hearing the captain's report they asked where Hsiao-hsi had gone. Others told them he had hidden in Li's house and then run away.

They discussed how to deal with the ten men, and finally agreed to hand them over to the district head. However they insisted that later, when they caught Hsiao-hsi, he must be shot in front of all the villagers. District Head Wang took the ten deserters back to the county government, and after being disciplined they were drafted into the army again.

Hsiao-hsi had led ten men out to plunder, but lost both men and rifles. Not daring return to White Dragon Temple to face his chief, he went to the town and looked up Fatty Wei, and joined the puppet committee as a running dog of the Japanese. Later he led the Japanese mounted patrol several times to the village to make trouble, frightening the villagers so that they fled to the mountains. Old Wang's grocery was burned. Chun-hsi was called to town to work for the Japanese, and a puppet committee was organized in the village with Li as its head and Little Mao as messenger. After this, it was not safe for members of the Self Defence Corps and young wives to stay at home. Every month the villagers had to send pigs, goats and white flour to the Japanese in the town, and when the enemy and traitors came to the village they demanded good food and women.

11

BECAUSE HE WAS TOO OLD TO MOVE ABOUT QUICKLY through open country with the others, Old Wang hid in a relative's house in a mountain village seven or eight miles away. The name of this village was Mountain-Back, and the enemy had never been there, so whenever the Japanese started combing the neighbourhood of the highway for partisans, the latter would often lie low here for a day or so.

One day Tieh-so and Leng-yuan arrived, and in answer to Wang's questions about conditions in the village, Leng-yuan said: "Don't talk of it! The village is in the clutches of Li and Little Mao again! The families of some of the Self Defence Corps have already paid the emergency tax, and their old folk have told them to come home to live. There are only about a dozen of us from the Sacrifice League who would rather die than support the puppet regime, and who are on the move all the time with the seven rifles of the Self Defence Corps. It's late spring, the autumn crops have all been planted here, but down our way apart from a few fields of wheat all the rest is still covered with maize. The Japanese keep coming every other day. They've killed and eaten all the farm animals, so we're not the only ones who can't sow: even those who've paid the emergency tax have to act as porters for the enemy every two or three days, leaving them no time for their own work...."

When Wang heard this his heart sank, and he wondered how long this would go on. Both Little Chang and District Head Wang had counselled endurance, yet all one could see was the savagery of the enemy, no movement on the part of our side. What good could come of such endurance? He asked Tieh-so if Little Chang or District Head Wang had visited them recently.

"District Head Wang came once," said Tieh-so. "He said it's because the previous mobilization was not well done that we're so weak now. But with these few rifles and men we can steadily resist the enemy and the traitors, and in the course of fighting gradually increase our own strength."

After they had left, Wang stayed awake all night thinking. But no matter how hard he thought, he could see no hope and no good end to such a state of affairs. He was an impatient person, and once he had an idea always wanted to act on it immediately, so the next morning he decided to go and find Little Chang.

Little Chang and the other comrades of the county branch of the Sacrifice League were living in the same village as the county government, some fifteen miles or so from Mountain-Back. Wang did not know the way, and he was after all an old fellow of sixty, so it took him a whole day to walk those fifteen miles. The sun was nearly setting when he came to a small mountain village and saw ahead other villages from which smoke was pouring as if they were on fire. When he asked, he was told that troops had arrived and lit fires to cook their food: people from this village had just returned from sending them firewood. When he inquired what troops these were, the villagers did not know. They could only tell him there were a great many, enough to fill several villages, and the county government had ordered all the neighbouring villages to send firewood. Although he could not get clear answers to his questions, Old Wang decided since the county government had ordered firewood to be sent these must be Chinese troops. Accordingly he asked where the county government was staying, and when the villagers had pointed out the place he went on.

By the time he reached his destination it was dark. There were troops quartered in every house and every courtyard, but after great difficulty he discovered the building occupied by the Sacrifice League, and found Little Chang. Little Chang was talking to some soldiers about getting volunteers to serve as stretcher-bearers, and could not see in the dark who it was; and Wang, unwilling to interrupt him, sat down in the court to wait. Presently Little Chang saw the others off. On his return, seeing there was still someone in the courtyard, he walked toward Wang and recognized him from his beard, glasses and walking stick.

"Well! Old Comrade!" he exclaimed, grasping his hand. "How did you get here?"

But just then more soldiers came to look for him, so he asked some other comrades to take Wang inside and see that he had a wash and a meal, while he talked with the new arrivals. However, before the soldiers had left, the county government summoned him to a meeting. All the other comrades were busy with their own work, so after Wang had finished his meal he had to lie down and wait. It was nearly midnight when Little Chang came back. When Wang heard the door open, he sat up and said, "Are you back? How busy you are!"

"Aren't you asleep yet, Comrade?" said Little Chang. "Aren't you tired?"

Wang got up and moved over to sit by the table, while Little Chang turned up the lamp and sat down too, asking: "What did you want to see me about? How have things been recently at the village?"

"That's what I came about," said Wang. "The village is entirely in the hands of the puppets, with Landlord Li as chairman and Little Mao as his running dog."

"That much I know," said Little Chang. "We've had a report. What new developments have there been?"

"There haven't been many developments," said Wang, "but things are bad enough as it is. It will soon be May, but not a grain of wheat has been sown there...."

"Don't you worry, Comrade!" said Little Chang. "Let me give you a piece of good news: the 108th

Japanese Division, which attacked southeast Shansi from nine sides wanting to wipe out our anti-Japanese resistance, has been annihilated by the Eighth Route Army. These troops from the Eighth Route Army who came today are here to take back this part. There is already one detachment ready to attack down your way. Very soon your district will be retaken."

"Is it true?" demanded Wang loudly.

"Of course it's true," answered Little Chang. "I shall be leaving too tomorrow morning, to help them organize the stretcher-bearers."

"In that case," said Wang, "can I go back with you to our village to help out?"

"Old Comrade!" said Little Chang. "Don't be so impatient! You're old, and you've spent a whole day walking: you don't need to go back tomorrow. If you wait a day or so until the fighting is over, you can go back after the enemy has been driven out. The village business can be left to Tieh-so and the others who are there." But although he reasoned with him for some time, Wang still insisted, so Little Chang had to give in.

That night Little Chang slept like a log, but Old Wang was too happy to sleep at all. Once the Japanese were driven away, he was sure the next step would be to arrest the traitors—they would certainly arrest Hsiao-hsi and Chun-hsi in town, and Li and Little Mao in the village. "Let's see if you can wriggle out of this, Li!" he gloated. The more he thought the more wide awake he felt, and the livelier grew his imagination. He pictured how the battle would be fought, how the Japanese would run, what a sorry figure Li would cut after his arrest, how Little Mao would kowtow and beg for mercy, and how the villagers would curse them.... One picture succeeded another in his mind, and only at cockcrow did he fall asleep.

This was just the time for the troops to eat. Little Chang got up and, having finished his breakfast before it was light, set out with the troops. By the time Old Wang got up the sun had almost risen. When the other comrades told him Little Chang had left, and urged him to stay for another day or two before going back, he was very upset. He blamed Little Chang for not calling him, and wanted to set out after him immediately; but the others told him he would never catch up, and that if he insisted on leaving he must first eat something, because he would find no food on the road. While they were talking the food arrived, so he forced himself to swallow a little rice, still determined to leave, and then said good-bye to the league comrades. But instead of making for Mountain-Back, he headed straight for home.

A journey of over twenty miles through the mountains takes even young people a day, but this old fellow must have had unusual stamina, for by midday he had caught up with the troops. The file of soldiers was so long, however, it stretched ahead of him however fast he hurried, and he could not find Little Chang. As he neared home he found all the villages within a radius of one or two miles occupied by troops. After stumbling several miles through the dark he reached Li Village. There were soldiers in the temple, soldiers in the watch house. All his houses but one had been burnt by the enemy, and in that one his whole family was crowded: wife, children, daughters-in-law and grandchildren. Yet even here the outer room was filled with soldiers. However, instead of going to his own home first, he went straight to find Tieh-so. There was no difficulty about that: Tieh-so's three-roomed house which had formerly been a stable had not been burnt by the Japanese and had no soldiers in it: there was straw spread on the floor, and Little Chang was staying here. When District Head Wang arrived he put up here too.

When Little Chang saw that Old Wang had arrived back, he thoroughly admired his spirit, and at once urged him to lie down and rest.

In answer to his questions, Tieh-so told him: "They say the Japanese have evacuated the city. This evening the villages along the highway have been occupied by our troops too. They will probably start fighting before it is light tomorrow. The village stretchers are ready."

"Doesn't the enemy know our troops are here?" asked Wang.

"No," said Tieh-so. "This afternoon, before the main force arrived, a small detachment came ahead to seal up the road in front. Nobody is allowed to pass, whoever he is."

Presently Wang's son came to fetch him home for a meal, but he said: "You bring the food here! There are other things I want to ask about."

When the food had been brought, Tieh-so said: "Why don't you let your father sleep here? Your house is packed full!"

Wang's son agreed, and went back again to fetch some bedding.

For some time all had been bustle and confusion. Now they were just going to sleep when several soldiers came running in, and one asked: "Is the village head here?"

"Yes," said Tieh-so.

"Come and see if this is a good man or not," said another. "In the middle of the night at the third watch he was skirting the road, hurrying toward the town!"

When Tieh-so went out he saw it was Little Mao, and said to the soldier: "A traitor! A traitor! Running dog of the puppet government!"

"Then we'll send him to Headquarters," said the soldier.

"Tieh-so, Tieh-so!" pleaded Little Mao desperately, "I—I—I—was hiding out! I...."

"Get moving, get moving!" said the soldier, and dragged him off.

When Old Wang heard Little Mao's voice he wanted to go out and see him, but hearing that he had already been taken off, he said to himself: "Little Mao! See where you've landed yourself? Let's see if you can get out of this or not!" Little Chang and District Head Wang both knew what Little Mao was and realized he was not being unjustly treated, so they asked no questions but went to sleep. Little Mao's arrest reminded Old Wang of Li, but Tieh-so told him Li was under surveillance, and with this assurance he went to sleep.

Old Wang had been walking for two days and had not slept properly for two nights, so when he lay down that evening without taking his clothes off he immediately fell sound asleep, only to be woken at the fifth watch the next morning by the sound of the first shells. It was still dark, but a lamp had been lit, and Little Chang, District Head Wang and Tieh-so had left. In late spring it is still cold at the fifth watch, so they had covered him with an extra quilt. Erh-niu had got up some time ago and was sitting on the bed, while the child beside her had been woken up too by the shells.

"Can't you sleep any more, Mr. Wang?" said Erh-niu. "Listen! The guns are firing: they have started fighting!"

"Mother!" exclaimed the boy. "What are you talking about? What fighting?"

"I'm talking about those soldiers who stayed here last night," said Erh-niu. "They've gone to the highroad to fight the Japanese!"

Immediately after this they heard two shells, and Wang stood up and said: "I'm going out to listen!" Then he went out.

"Mother," said the boy, "let's go out to listen too." He promptly put on his clothes and went out with Erh-niu.

The young and able-bodied had already left with the army, some as stretcher-bearers, some as guides. A number of women and children and old men had come out onto the street to listen to the firing, but it was still fairly quiet. When the sound of shells became more frequent, Old Wang with some of the more curious hurriedly climbed the hill outside the village for a better view; because with the hill in their way they could not see from what direction the firing came, but could only see flashes in the sky and hear the sound of machine guns and rifles. At first they only heard firing from the south, then it spread to the southwest. By the time it was light things were becoming more and more lively, the sound of rifles and guns intermingling. Presently firing started in the west too, mingling with the sounds in the south and southwest over a distance of about ten miles. It was now quite bright, and all the villagers who had not gone to the front with the troops climbed hills around the village to listen. Only when it was time for breakfast did the sound of firing gradually die away. By this time some had gone home to prepare food, while others stayed on the hill trying to guess what was happening.

Suddenly a detachment of soldiers appeared in the southwest valley, but it was impossible to make out whether they were enemy troops or our own. The villagers panicked and ran to their hiding places, and when those who had gone home to cook heard this news they all hurried into hiding too. Only when the soldiers left by the brigade told them these were their own troops coming back did they come out again.

Troops, stretcher-bearers and Self Defence Corps had returned together. The enemy had been completely routed, several hundred killed and four cars destroyed. Many trophies had been taken: Japanese horses, steel helmets, rifles, uniforms, car wheels, iron rods.... The wounded were not taken down from their stretchers, but after being given something to eat were sent on immediately to the rear, the remainder of the troops staying in the surrounding villages to rest.

The brigade handed over Li and Little Mao to District Head Wang to deal with, and the villagers were one and all in favour of executing them, giving their families such a fright that they kowtowed fast and hard. Later it was agreed not to execute them but insist on their making good all the losses they had caused the village by entertaining the enemy. If only their lives were spared the two men did not mind losing all their property. The authorities proposed that in addition to making good any losses, they must also reform completely and promise never to act as traitors again, and this too the villagers approved. After this decision District Head Wang sent them to the county government to be dealt with.

After the county seat was recaptured, the county government returned to the town. When Li and Little Mao were handed over to the county government, Little Mao was so afraid of being killed that he confessed to most of the crimes he had committed during the last ten years or so in the village with Li, Hsiao-hsi, Chun-hsi and the like.

Unfortunately, when the Japanese retreated from the town, Hsiao-hsi and Chun-hsi had fled with Fatty Wei and his group to take refuge with Detachment Commander Tien. The county government ordered their return, but Commander Tien would not give them up, and sent back an official letter justifying them, claiming that they had been sent to the puppet government as secret service agents. The county government had Little Mao's clear and detailed statement as to how Hsiao-hsi had brought the bandits to the village to dig up the cave, guided the Japanese to burn houses, arrest people and set up a puppet office, and taken Chun-hsi to the city to become a traitor. But Commander Tien absolutely refused to give them up, and the government representatives returned from all their negotiations empty-handed. Commander Tien, with force on his side, would not give way; and the county government, with right on its side, would not give way either. Finally both sides acted independently—Commander Tien continued to shelter the two men, while the county government confiscated their property.

During the two months they spent in the county seat Li and Little Mao confessed to their crimes and agreed to make reparation, after which the county government sent a section chief with District Head Wang to escort them back to the village for a mass trial. According to Li's estimate in the county seat, they had given the Japanese four pigs, ten cows and less than a thousand catties of white flour. This he and Little Mao could make good by handing over some livestock, without selling any property. But once they got back it was a different story.

The section chief and District Head Wang told them to repeat to the whole community what they had confessed in the county seat, whereupon Little Mao started to describe all they had done during the last ten years to oppress the masses as, for instance, when Chun-hsi cheated Tieh-so. In over a dozen cases they had made use of the office of village head to ruin families on flimsy pretexts, and to squeeze an incalculable amount of money out of the villagers. The mention of these old wrongs aroused the anger of the masses, so that with clenched fists and glaring eyes they insisted on settling old scores with Li. And he, for his part, was so afraid of being beaten that he confessed to everything. As a result they decided it was not enough for Li to forfeit all his property, and the section chief had to plead for him before the villagers would consent to leave him one house. Little Mao usually just ate and drank with Li and his group without making a great deal of money, moreover he had confessed very fully, so it was decided simply to fine him several piculs of millet to be given to the Self Defence Corps for training purposes. All Hsiao-hsi and Chun-hsi's property was confiscated until such time as they should come back to stand trial.

12

THE ENEMY HAD FLED, LANDLORD LI HAD FALLEN, Chun-hsi and Hsiao-hsi had gone, and Little Mao had learnt a lesson and would never dare make trouble again. The village became a hive of industry—Workers', Peasants', Women's and Young People's National Salvation Leagues were set up, together with a People's Night School and Dramatic Troupe. The Self Defence Corps started training again, buying new ammunition and hand grenades....

And everybody dared speak out. Much of Hsiao-hsi and Chun-hsi's property had been unjustly seized from others, and, after it had been sealed up for over a month without any sentence against them being passed, some villagers proposed that those parts which had been unjustly seized should be returned to the rightful owners, the remainder awaiting the government's decision. Tieh-so as village head accepted the people's views and reported them to

District Head Wang, who reported them in turn to the county government.

One day District Head Wang went to the county seat to follow up this matter, and the county magistrate said to him: "Here's a pretty kettle of fish! They must have complained to Commander Yen that the county government confiscated their property on some trumped-up charge, because now Commander Yen has sent a telegram reprimanding me, ordering that their property be returned to them." Saying this, he showed him the telegram.

"Everybody knows the way those two carried on in the village," said District Head Wang. "Besides there is Little Mao's confession for complete confirmation; how can they deny it? I think you might send all that evidence to the garrison headquarters and see what they can say then."

"I thought of that too," said the county magistrate, "only since the authorities already believe their side of the story and have reprimanded me, it shows they are prejudiced in their favour. So I'm afraid sending the evidence won't make any difference. Still, that's the right thing to do. The county government can't protect traitors and try to cover up crimes of which we already have proof."

When District Head Wang went back he told Tieh-so, and Tieh-so went back to tell the whole village, throwing everyone into a ferment. Protesting indignantly, and without waiting to be summoned, more and more people gathered round the gate of the watch house and started holding a meeting. They passed a resolution that the leading cadres of the

Workers', Peasants', Women's and Young People's Leagues should lead them to the county government to make a demonstration. The next day, accordingly, they organized over two hundred demonstrators, who took provisions with them to the county seat. The county magistrate knew the truth of the matter, and when the villagers had completely surrounded the county government he explained the situation to them, at the same time sending a telegram to Commander Yen. Two days later Commander Yen's reply arrived, instructing him to take no action until his representative had investigated the matter.

When the villagers returned home they prepared material in readiness for the inspector's coming, but for weeks they waited in vain. Then, after over a month the opium commissioner arrived. (At that time every county had an official in charge of the sale of official opium, whose title was economic commissioner, but the people called him opium commissioner.) Everybody knew what this official had come for, and that it would be no use talking to him, so they did not think it worth while to take it up with him. However, he insisted on going through the empty forms, and asked Tieh-so to convene a public meeting for discussion. In the meeting he started making a speech. He made up a story to excuse Hsiao-hsi and Chun-hsi, saying the peasants did not understand secret service work in the army, that these two had been sent by the Tien Detachment into the enemy's lair to spy out conditions there.

At this point Pai-kou interrupted him to say: "Economic Commissioner! I know all about that!"

The commissioner supposed he understood the meaning of secret service, and thought he would enlist his support.

"Oh, do you?" he said. Then to the others: "Let him speak!"

"Hsiao-hsi was an old hand at secret service work," said Pai-kou.

"Right!" put in the commissioner.

Some people were afraid Pai-kou had not realized that the commissioner was simply lying on behalf of Hsiao-hsi and Chun-hsi, and thought he was playing into his hands, so they were displeased at his interrupting.

But Pai-kou went on: "He really was an old hand! First he did secret service work among the bandits at White Dragon Mountain, guiding ten of them to our village to dig up caves and finding the grocery's cave in no time. Then he went to town to do secret service work there, guiding the enemy to our village to burn property, reducing the grocery to cinders in no time. Only an old hand could do things so quickly and competently."

Before he had finished there was a burst of laughter from the crowd, and cries of "Quite right!" The commissioner wanted to stop him, but since he himself had asked him to speak he could not think of a good reason to silence him, and while he was racking his brains Pai-kou had already said so much.

And no sooner had Pai-kou finished than Leng-yuan started: "You're only talking of the present, you haven't mentioned the past! Earlier on Hsiao-hsi...."

"Wait a bit!" said the commissioner. "Listen! I haven't finished speaking yet!"

"If you hadn't finished, why should Pai-kou speak?" interrupted others.

"Did you come to make an investigation or to practise speaking?"

"You know more than we do about selling opium, but you don't know as much as we do about Hsiao-hsi and Chun-hsi."

"If you know more than we do, what are you investigating?"

Finally someone called out: "Let's all go, and leave him to instruct himself!" Thereupon they started rushing noisily away.

Seeing the embarrassing position the commissioner was in, Tieh-so went up to the platform and shouted: "The commissioner hasn't finished speaking: don't go yet!"

The villagers shouted back: "If he hasn't finished let him take his time! We've no time to listen!"

Shouting and jeering they went away, about a dozen halting some way off to see how the commissioner would take this. Tieh-so called them to come back and listen, but the commissioner saw that the situation was hopeless, and said: "Never mind, never mind! The work here has really been disgracefully done, the people don't even know how to behave at a meeting!"

Tieh-so had been afraid that he would be overcome by embarrassment, little thinking he would blame the work in the village, so he retorted: "Country people all speak straight out, and only say what they think. I hope you will make allowances for them."

The official had no way of venting his anger, but after dinner went to see Landlord Li. Although Li had lost his land, he had not yet stopped smoking opium, and knowing the commissioner was an addict too he lit the lamp and invited him to lie down. The commissioner asked who had reported Hsiao-hsi and Chun-hsi to the county government, and said: "The county government is using Little Mao's confession as evidence. What kind of person is this Little Mao?"

"He used to be under us," said Li, and explained Little Mao's background to him. The commissioner then told him to send someone to fetch Little Mao, and Li sent his son.

Little Mao felt it was because he had said too much in the county seat that Li had lost his houses and property. He had long wanted to apologize, but fearing the villagers would accuse him of calling on Li to make mischief, he had never dared go. During the meeting that day he realized that the commissioner was protecting Hsiao-hsi and Chun-hsi, and was eager to talk it over with him, but he felt it would be presumptuous to trouble him. And since the villagers dared laugh at the commissioner openly, they would treat him with even less ceremony: so again he dared not go. Now this unexpected summons seemed an opportunity to kill two birds with one stone: firstly he could apologize to Li, and secondly he could see the official. Naturally he was delighted, and jumped up as if he were on springs to go back with the messenger.

When he entered Li's house and saw the commissioner and Li lying on the same bed smoking opium, he knew the official was on their side, and felt even bolder.

"This is Little Mao!" said Li.

The commissioner looked at him and said: "So you are Little Mao? Sit down!" Saying this he drew up his legs to make room for him on a corner of the bed, and Little Mao slipped across and sat down. "Little Mao!" said the commissioner, "Mr. Li tells me you are very able: then why couldn't you look after yourself when you were away from home?"

Little Mao did not understand, and said: "It's a long time since I was away from home."

"I'm not talking of the last few days," said the commissioner with a smile. "I'm talking of when you were in the county seat. When you were in town what nonsense did you tell them?"

Little Mao realized what he meant, and started lamenting: "Good sir! Think when that was! My life was in danger! How could I say what I wanted?"

"You really have no guts," said the commissioner. "If that side can take your life, do you suppose this side can't? All the members of the Sacrifice League are Communists, the county magistrate and district head both belong to the Sacrifice League, so naturally they are Communists too. They eat at Commander Yen's expense, but they don't do what he wants, and in future he will have them arrested. Hsiao-hsi and Chun-hsi and even Mr. Li here are all loyal to the commander. You listened to the Communists and injured Commander Yen's men, so in future when the commander liquidates Communists, won't you be dealt with too?"

Little Mao had been very happy when he came, but hearing the commissioner talk like this he began to be afraid, and said pleadingly: "Sir, you see things so clearly, while we common people are in the dark! However, the mistake has already been made, so I must ask you to help me! It wasn't that I wanted to go along with them, but they really forced me so that I had no alternative!" Saying this he shed tears.

"Don't be afraid," said the commissioner. "Since you made a mistake you must make good that mistake! You had better write a recantation, which I will take back and send in to the commander's headquarters; then there will be no trouble for you later. Not only will you be cleared, but provided you work loyally for Mr. Li, Hsiao-hsi and Chun-hsi, later when they have power again they will find some job for you."

"Since you are so good to me, sir," said Little Mao, "I can't say how grateful I am. But how shall I write this recantation? I'm an ignorant fellow, and know nothing. I must ask you to help me a little."

"That's very easy," said the commissioner. "Just say they were Communists wanting to spread Communism. They used trumped-up charges to confiscate rich people's property, and forced you to sign your name to a confession they had already prepared. If you write a short recantation like this, it will be good for you and good for Hsiao-hsi and the others too." Then he turned to Li: "Mr. Li! I think you had better write this for him!"

"Very well!" said Li.

"I really ought to invite you to a meal to show my thanks," said Little Mao. "Sir, don't go tomorrow, but let me express my great gratitude!"

"That's not necessary," said the commissioner. "The Communists have too many ears in your village, we mustn't give them a chance to throw mud at us. Later on we shall have plenty of occasions for meeting: this doesn't matter!"

So this was how the investigation was carried out. Li wrote a recantation for Little Mao, which the commissioner took with him the next day and forwarded to Commander Yen's office. The villagers knew that when the opium commissioner went back he would not have a good word to say for them; but they would just have to wait for further orders from above.

On his return the commissioner wrote a report of his investigation and sent it together with the recantation to Commander Yen's headquarters. The main theme of his report was that this case had been entirely fabricated by the Communists, because Hsiao-hsi and Chun-hsi had both been officers during the period of anti-Communist resistance—Hsiao-hsi as captain of the Anti-Communist Guard and Chun-hsi as captain of the Righteous Brigade. Because of this the Communists in the village and county had made use of their political power and mass organization to frame them as traitors and divide up their property.

This was the time when the Eighth Route Army in Shansi was everywhere defeating the Japanese, recapturing lost territory and setting up centres of anti-Japanese resistance; while the Shansi-Suiyuan Kuomintang army had retreated to the Yellow River in southwest Shansi, not daring to penetrate behind the enemy lines. Yen Hsi-shan was worried, and mortally afraid lest his officers cooperate with the Communists. His Dare-to-Die Corps had learnt guerilla tactics and political leadership from the Eighth Route Army, and he considered them virtually Communists already. In his view Shansi belonged to him, and all comers ought to act as "filial sons." Now, however, he saw many places that his filial sons had been unable to hold taken by the Japanese, and while his filial sons could not recapture these places they were recaptured by the Eighth Route Army. Naturally he was worried. And just at this time every district had traitors who had been sentenced (rogues like Chun-hsi), but refused to admit that they were traitors and insisted that their accusers wanted to divide up their property. Administrative officials and captains of the Righteous Brigade who had been frightened away by the Japanese would not admit that they had been scared out of their wits, but insisted that the Sacrifice League was hand in glove with the Eighth Route Army to wrest their power from them. And all complained to Commander Yen. Yen Hsi-shan realized that these men were mortal enemies of Communism, so he selected some of the more able ones and summoned them by telegram, to train them as a new group of "filial sons." Hsiao-hsi and Chun-hsi were among this group. He also sent Commander Tien to southeast Shansi to form troops like the Tien Detachment into an independent Eighth

Brigade as a nucleus for a future attack on the Communists.

After the confiscation of Hsiao-hsi and Chun-hsi's property, because no sentence was passed the land grew wild. The villagers pressed the county government for a decision several times, and were told another request had been made to the authorities for Hsiao-hsi and Chun-hsi's return to stand trial. They waited and waited until the summer was over; but the authorities, far from sending Hsiao-hsi and Chun-hsi back, summoned them to headquarters. The villagers waited and waited again, until the enemy started a second offensive, when they were so busy preparing to fight that they shelved the question. This time Li, Little Mao and their ilk did not dare organize any puppet committee. Enemy patrols came several times, but two of them were shot dead by the Self Defence Corps, and the Japanese went back without coming into the village, so the peasants suffered no losses. When the 344th Brigade of the Eighth Route Army had driven the enemy out again, the villagers once more brought up the question of Hsiao-hsi and Chun-hsi's property. Fresh enquiries at the county government elicited the answer that an official reply had been received to the effect that the two men were loyal officers and Little Mao's confession had been forced out of him. His recantation was enclosed with the official letter.

This roused the villagers to fury. They immediately called a public meeting and had Little Mao tied up. Then some youngsters brandished hoes over his head and said: "Since we have the reputation of forcing confessions out of people, let's force another! Go on! What was false in your first confession?"

Little Mao kept his eyes on the hoes, not daring to look the men in the face, too frightened to say a single word.

The whole crowd shouted: "Make him speak!"

Little Mao was afraid if he did not speak he would be beaten, so kowtowing he stuttered, "It was all t-t-true!"

"Who told you to write a recantation?" someone asked.

"The commissioner!" said Little Mao.

"Who wrote it for you?" asked another.

When Little Mao did not dare say, a youngster gave him a blow on his behind, and he let out a yell.

"Hurry up and tell us!" they insisted. "Who wrote it for you?"

Little Mao felt it was more than his life was worth to keep silent, so he said trembling: "Li-Li-Li...!" The hoe over his head had to move before he would complete Landlord Li's name.

"How did the commissioner come to ask you to write a recantation?" asked Leng-yuan. "What did he say to you? How is it you were willing?"

"I had to write it!" said Little Mao. "The commissioner said that side would have my life!" He went on to describe how he had seen the commissioner that evening.

Leng-yuan jumped onto the platform and called out: "You've all heard! Everything in the confession was true, the commissioner made him write a recantation, and that old traitor Li saw to writing it for him! What monkey business is this? In my opinion we'd better decide ourselves what to do with Hsiao-hsi and Chun-hsi's property: let whatever was tricked out of people be returned to the original owners, and the rest become the public property of the village! It doesn't matter what government, commissioner, commander it is—whoever comes we'll tell him the truth! Even if the King of Heaven comes we're not afraid of him! Unless he won't hear a word of the truth, and sends soldiers to wipe out this village of ours!"

With raised fists they all shouted their approval. But Tieh-so said: "A trial like this seems perfectly fair here in our village, but how can we report it to the authorities? Of course the county government knows the truth of the situation, unfortunately since that opium commissioner's investigation and Little Mao's recantation the rights and wrongs have all been mixed up. How can the county government explain it to the higher authorities?"

"When that opium commissioner came," said Old Yang, "he wouldn't let us speak. He spent a night in Li's place and fixed up that recantation with Little Mao, then left. What kind of investigation is that? As I see it, if an official can play such dirty tricks then we as common people can bring a charge against him, saying his investigation was false and asking the authorities to make another investigation, insisting on the real truth being known." Everybody approved.

"I have a proposal," said Pai-kou. "Since Little Mao wrote a false recantation for the commissioner, he can write a true one for us. Let's make him write out truthfully how he saw the commissioner that evening, and we can send it to Commander Yen. Then see what they have to say!"

They all clapped and said: "Right! Make him write at once!"

But Little Mao said he could not write, so they had to find someone to write for him. Old Wang, who was chosen, felt a little uneasy, and said: "In ordinary circumstances anybody would be willing to write. But nothing would induce me to write this! In the first place I'm deputy village head, so it is not proper for me to write. In the second place, they are too clever at cheating people! To play their dirty game someone had to have the idea, and someone had to write: if he could write that, why can't he write this?"

Pai-kou realized what he meant and said: "Right! Let's drag Li out and make him write! Make Little Mao say a sentence and Li write a sentence. If he refuses we'll send him to the county government to find out what mischief he was up to with the commissioner and Little Mao, to ask the traitor what he confessed and why he still writes things for traitors to cheat honest people."

Again the whole group applauded, while some youngsters had already dashed off to fetch Li. When Li knew that they wanted him to write down what had happened the night the commissioner stayed with him, it was obviously writing a charge against himself and of course he would not do it. Finally the villagers pushed him down and beat him, then sent him in to the county government with Little Mao.

Regarding the property of the two cousins, Tieh-so said: "Not to wait at all for official instructions is not good. We'd better first return the property they tricked out of people to the original owners to cultivate, and leave the rest sealed up until the case is finally settled."

The young men were still in favour of deciding at once, but Old Chen said: "First restore part of the land to its rightful owners, and leave the rest till instructions come. It will take some time for the case to be settled." Eventually everyone agreed to this.

They waited till after New Year, but still no official instructions came. When they made careful enquiries they learned that Commander Yen had fled across the Yellow River to Shensi, and beyond this there was no further news.

13

WHEN THE TIME FOR SOWING CAME IN SPRING THE villagers would wait no longer for orders from above, but by the decree of the village administration office the land unjustly acquired by Li, Hsiao-hsi and Chunhsi was returned to the original owners who sowed crops there. That year the harvest was not bad, so the families unjustly bankrupted by Li and his nephews could live decently again—Tieh-so harvested over twenty piculs of grain, and Little Fatty was able to stop minding cattle for other people and come back to the village to attend school.

The only thing that worried them all was that the authorities had still not issued any orders, and Li was still detained in the county seat. After they had pressed the matter several times the county government said: "Just carry out the sentence passed in your village, there ought not to be any trouble."

When Tieh-so went into town, Little Chang told him: "Yen Hsi-shan has recently called all his reactionary forces to Chiulin for a meeting, and is determined to attack the progressive forces of our Sacrifice League and the Dare-to-Die Corps: I'm afraid they will back Hsiao-hsi and his uncle to the limit in your village. The county government can't very well make any decision in this matter: better decide in the village, and if the county government doesn't contest it, consider it as settled."

In the eleventh month of the lunar calendar some Kuomintang soldiers suddenly came to the village and demanded accommodation, asking the village head for so much firewood and hay that Tieh-so could not meet all their demands. The next day the main body of troops arrived and ordered roads to be paved and the highway to be repaired, keeping the villagers so busy that they did not know whether they were on their heads or their heels. In the evening a fresh lot of people arrived. The first group included Chun-hsi, Thin Lips, Duck Neck and others who had been in Fifth Master's house that day. They called themselves the Spiritual Mobilization Committee (Yen Hsi-shan's secret service). The second group comprised a number of men with pistols, headed by Hsiao-hsi, calling themselves Commandos (another of Yen Hsi-shan's secret service organizations in army uniform). As soon as Leng-yuan and Tieh-so saw them they knew there was going to be trouble, and privately took counsel with several of the most active members of the Sacrifice League as to how to meet this situation.

"I think you'd better send someone to make enquiries at the county government, at the same time going into hiding yourselves," said Old Wang. "You can leave the work of the village administration office to me for the time being, and I'll look after them. An old fellow like myself can turn a deaf ear to them, and they can't do anything to me."

"It's obvious they're here for no good," said the others. "If we're to hide, let's all hide, why should you stay here to bear the brunt?"

Wang disagreed, saying, "If they really want to make trouble, the worst that can happen is for me to die, and how much longer should I live anyway?" He insisted on staying behind. Tieh-so, Leng-yuan and a dozen other leaders thereupon went into hiding, taking with them the rifles of the Self Defence Corps. Only Pai-kou, who had been wounded when fighting with the regular troops against the Japanese in the autumn, was unable to leave. He had to stay at home to await events.

The men who left took refuge in Mountain-Back Village where Old Wang had formerly stayed, sending Leng-yuan to the county government to ask for advice. After many hours Leng-yuan came back saying: "We're done for! Comrade Little Chang has been buried alive by them!" And saying this he broke down. The others were absolutely aghast, and immediately started asking questions. Presently Leng-yuan controlled himself enough to tell them: "The day before yesterday in the evening the Kuomintang troops and Commandos surrounded the county government and Sacrifice League. Some of the people inside fought their way out, some were killed in the fighting, some were arrested and killed, and some are still being arrested. No one knows whether the county magistrate is alive or dead! Comrade Little Chang was buried alive!" When he said this they all shed tears. Asked who had told him, he said it was a messenger of the Sacrifice League who had escaped. After this news they realized they would not be able to go home. The neighbouring villages were swarming with Kuomintang troops, Spiritual Mobilization Committees and Commandos. They had very little provisions or money with them, and all they could do was to move from place to place in the mountains. When asked what regiment they belonged to, they said they were guerillas.

After wandering about for four or five days they reached a mountain village where they found Erh-niu and her eleven-year-old boy begging. They called her to the sunniest slope and asked what had happened in the village.

Erh-niu wrung her hands and said, "I can't talk of it! Everything's finished! They arrested over a hundred people, saying they were Communists. Some had their hands cut off, some their eyes gouged out, some their money taken.... The courtyard of Dragon King Temple flowed with blood, you had to walk through blood." Then she told them how many people had been killed. When they heard they just shook their heads.

"We thought apart from the dozen of us the others would be all right," said Leng-yuan. "Who could have imagined that people like Tsui Hei-hsiao, who can't even talk, would be killed by them too. The bloody butchers!"

Tieh-so noticed that Erh-niu had not included Old Wang's name among those killed, so asked what had become of him. "The old fellow was seized and taken into the temple," said Erh-niu, "and they insisted that he confess to having committed crimes.

" 'Since you are so good at killing, hurry up and kill me!' said Old Wang. 'What crimes have I committed? I ought not to have helped poor people! I ought not to have refused to be a traitor! I can't think of anything else! You choose any crimes you like!'

"Landlord Li has come back to be village head and Little Mao is deputy head. They said Old Wang must be killed. But in the end some of the old people in the Li family knelt to them and pleaded: 'Don't be so cruel! He's over sixty years old!' So they allowed him to pay five thousand silver dollars to save his life."

When they asked about Pai-kou, Erh-niu cried. "They treated Pai-kou terribly," she said. "I don't know whether he'll live or not! The day that they arrested people Hsiao-hsi went himself to arrest Pai-kou. He told Pai-kou to get up and walk, but the wounds in his leg weren't better and he couldn't walk, so Hsiao-hsi slashed with a bayonet twice at his good leg, until trousers, socks, bed and floor were all spattered with blood. Finally he sent two men to carry Pai-kou bleeding as he was to the temple, and had my grandfather and father tied up too. The next day while Hsiao-hsi was busy killing other people he sent someone to Chiao-chiao to say if she would sleep with him for a month she could save the lives of her family. Chiao-chiao couldn't hide herself and at last they carried her off. That devil slept with her one night, then luckily his wife came out and made a scene—his wife is a niece of Li's wife, and can't be ignored, so he decided to give up Chiao-chiao."

"Why did you and the boy run away?" asked Tieh-so. "Did they want to kill you too? What have they done to our home?"

"Don't talk about a home any more!" said Erh-niu. "What home do we have? They said you were the leading Communist in our village and the troops surrounded the village and searched a whole day for you, and when they couldn't find you they threw me and the boy out, and sealed up our door. I couldn't bring away clothes or food or a single thing.

" 'Where do you want me and the child to go?' I asked.

" 'Who cares?' said Hsiao-hsi. 'If you want to die you needn't go, if you want to live get as far away as you can!'

"Grandfather and Father and Mother all privately urged me: 'Take the child and go, and save your lives! Don't stay in the village! They aren't afraid of killing people!' So then I ran away with the boy!"

When Tieh-so heard this he clenched his teeth and said: "All right. Anyway that's a clean sweep!"

Each of the others asked after his own family, and Erh-niu told them all she knew. Some families had had their property confiscated, some had been arrested, some had paid out money, some of their cases had not been settled by the time she left.

As she was speaking someone on the mountain called out: "Hey! What regiment are you?"

Looking up they saw a number of soldiers above them, and, taken aback, said to themselves: "That's bad!"

Since they had been challenged they had to answer, and Leng-yuan shouted: "Guerillas!"

The men above called out again: "Send someone up here!" They were very close and there was no way of hiding. Leng-yuan was always ready to take the lead, so he said, "I'll go," handing his rifle as he spoke to someone else. The rest of them waited below and heard the sound of voices but could not catch what was being said. After a while Leng-yuan called out: "All come on up! It's the Eighth Route Army!" When they heard that, they could have jumped for joy, and hurried up together, Erh-niu and the child following. These men were some of the Eighth Route Army guerillas. There were only two or three hundred of them, they had stayed in the neighbourhood of Li Village before, and some of them they knew. When Tieh-so had explained to the captain why they were there and asked if they could join them, the soldiers naturally welcomed them heartily, and so this group joined the army.

Tieh-so also asked them to conduct Erh-niu and the child to a safe place, but the captain said: "West of the Pai-Chin highway and south of the Lin-Tun highway we have no regular troops at present. There are only the few hundred of us, and we are acting on orders to go to Pingsun County east of the highway. The Kuomintang armies have occupied Tsincheng and that district, and their chief aim is to mop up these small units of ours, so we can't go that way. We shall have to fight our way through north of Kaoping across the Japanese lines, and it wouldn't be easy for a woman and child to cross."

"You look after yourself!" said Erh-niu to Tieh-so. "Don't worry about me! I'll manage somehow round here with the boy! He can go on minding cattle after New Year, and I'll gradually find some work to do: we shan't starve! The Kuomintang armies and Li and his nephews aren't made of iron to last forever! When things change for the better again I can still go back!"

After a short rest the troops moved on, and so Tieh-so left his wife and son—Erh-niu and the boy watching them all the way down the mountain.

14

AFTER NEW YEAR ERH-NIU BEGGED HER WAY TO A ONE-family village where she found a place of refuge. The heads of this family were an old couple over fifty, who had only one child of twelve. They employed two labourers to cultivate the land and had three oxen and two donkeys. Seeing how much live-stock they had Erh-niu asked if they wanted a boy to look after the oxen, and the old man asked her story. She dared not tell him the truth, but said her home had been destroyed by the Japanese and her husband was dead, so she had had to leave. There was nobody in the old man's house to do odd jobs, so he kept Little Fatty to look after the cattle and Erh-niu to do the cooking.

It was in the depth of the mountain, and as long as the enemy did not come they heard nothing of any changes in the situation, so Erh-niu and her son stayed on there. After a year and a half, however, when it was getting on for summer, the situation changed so drastically that repercussions were felt even in this village. One day bandits came and plundered right and left—in addition to looting, they killed the old man and drove off the farm animals.

After such a disaster naturally Erh-niu and her son could not stay on there, and had to go to look for work elsewhere. She set out again with Little Fatty to beg for a living. But when she reached another village and made enquiries, she heard that the Kuomintang Seventh Army in Chungtiao Mountain had been utterly routed by the enemy, and her home had again become one of the puppet villages. About two miles from Li Village the enemy had built a gun emplacement, the mountains for thirty miles around were filled with disbanded troops robbing and kidnapping wherever they went, and there was not a peaceful spot anywhere.

Hereupon Erh-niu made a new plan. She felt since all places were equally dangerous, the best thing would be to go home to have a look. If she went home she could see her family, there were no more Kuomintang troops, and there might still be some old furniture in the house she could sell. With this intention she set out with her son for home. When they were four or five miles from Li Village they saw two people on the mountain path—a man and a woman. The boy whose eyesight was good was soon able to recognize Pai-kou and Chiao-chiao, and said to Erh-niu: "Mother! Isn't that my uncle coming?" Erh-niu looked carefully and saw there was a resemblance. They risked calling out, and it was indeed Pai-kou and

Chiao-chiao, who came over to them. Pai-kou first asked Erh-niu where she had been for over a year, and how they had managed. Erh-niu told him, and also gave him the news that Tieh-so, Leng-yuan and the others had joined the Eighth Route Army.

"How right they were to run away!" said Pai-kou. "We people who stayed at home have had a terrible time of it for over a year!"

Erh-niu saw that he was wearing white shoes, and asked: "Who are you in mourning for?"

"What's the use of talking of it?" said Pai-kou. "During the past year the villagers have been having a dog's life of it. They demand porters, money, grain, hay, firewood, conscripts...not a day goes by without their demanding something! And if you happen to be at all slow they say you are an underground member of the Eighth Route Army deliberately resisting them! Last winter they fixed a tax which our father couldn't pay: he was given a beating and allowed two days to pay up in, driving him to jump off the cliff...." When Erh-niu heard this she could not help crying. And Pai-kou speaking of it broke down too. Presently Pai-kou went on: "When Father died, Grandfather fell ill of anger. I was afraid they would conscript me, so pretended that my legs hurt, going about limping. Last year we got a few piculs of grain but they were not satisfied with that, though our family of four had nothing to eat over New Year, and had to eat tree-leaves that made Grandfather's face swell."

"Where are you two off to now?" asked Erh-niu.

"Hah!" said Pai-kou. "So much has happened! That creature Hsiao-hsi has got as many lives as a cat!

When you left wasn't he captain in Yen Hsi-shan's secret service? Later all the posts in the county government and the district were filled by people sent by the Chiang Kai-shek army. Seeing Yen Hsi-shan's badge was no use any more, Chun-hsi and his group hurried back to join Yen, but Hsiao-hsi joined some work unit in the Chiang Kai-shek army. Every day he led some scoundrels to arrest "underground members of the Eighth Route Army," cheating people of money at every turn—anyone who had money was an underground member of the Eighth Route Army but once they paid up they were innocent again. You know, he was always coming to my house to make trouble!" Saying this he glanced at Chiao-chiao, and Chiao-chiao sighed and hung her head.

"When the Chiang Kai-shek troops were routed by the Japanese this time," Pai-kou went on, "Hsiao-hsi changed again—joined some Information Office in the Japanese army, still leading the same group of men, arresting people at every turn as underground members of the Eighth Route Army and cheating them of money. And whenever he comes back to the village he comes to my house to make trouble. Grandfather said, 'You find a place where she can hide. With creatures like this there's no end to it!' Old Wang is still living in Mountain-Back. I asked him to find a place, and he said, 'Bring her along!' That's where I'm taking her now!"

"Isn't that old devil Li dead yet?" asked Erh-niu.

"He's another with nine lives," said Pai-kou. "At the time you left he became village head again, and now he's the chief puppet official again!"

Erh-niu asked what had happened in the village after the Kuomintang troops left, and whether there was anything left in her house.

"Not a thing!" said Pai-kou. "Even the house where you lived was taken over by Chun-hsi to stable his mule!"

"Then why should I go back?" said Erh-niu. "Still, since I've come so far, I'll go back to see Mother and Grandfather!" And she said to the boy: "Little Fatty! You go with Uncle to Mountain-Back and wait for me! I'll go back to have a look and then come to fetch you! Anyway, the house is gone, and this way you won't have to run away if the Japanese come!" The boy agreed to go with Pai-kou and Chiao-chiao, and Erh-niu went on alone to the village.

As she walked she saw that things were different here from in the mountains—plot after plot of good level land had not been planted with seedlings, but weeds had grown over five feet high. Not a soul was in sight on the main road, which was overgrown with grass; and in the distance were only a few women and children with baskets gathering wild vegetables. When she reached the village, the streets there were overgrown with grass too, some of the houses had fallen into ruins and others were crumbling, while very few had doors or windows left. When she got back to the house they had lived in, the time was already past when Chun-hsi had stabled his mule there, and now even the dung behind the trough had dried up. The ground had been dug over several times, and was cluttered with ashes, decayed weeds, rubble and stones. When she went to her mother's house the courtyard there too was filled with brambles and weeds, with just a small path where people had trodden down the weeds. Her mother was in the court lighting a fire to cook a pan of ash-leaves, and when she saw Erh-niu without saying a word she burst into tears. After crying for a while mother and daughter went inside to see Old Chen, and cried and lamented together over more than a year's bitterness, until it was dark. There was nothing else in the house, so they closed the gate and made a meal off the leaves.

Before the bowls had been washed, they heard someone shouting fiercely outside: "Open the door!"

Erh-niu's mother jumped for fright, and said: "Hsiao-hsi!" And gave Erh-niu a push, saying: "Quick, hide under the bed!" So Erh-niu got under the bed.

"Why haven't you opened up yet?" called Hsiao-hsi impatiently.

"I'm just coming," said Erh-niu's mother. "I was asleep and have only just got up." Saying this she opened the door. Hsiao-hsi came in flashing his torch this way and that, and started walking straight to Chiao-chiao's room.

"They're not at home tonight," said Erh-niu's mother. "They've gone to visit her aunt!"

Hsiao-hsi flashed his torch onto the door, saw that it was locked, then exclaimed angrily: "Not there? Are you trying to trick me?" He picked up a brick, knocked off the padlock and went in to have a look, then came back to Old Chen's part of the house. With his torch he searched again all over the room, and when he flashed it under the bed and saw Erh-niu he took her for Chiao-chiao, and said, chuckling: "Come

193

out, come out! I've brought you some pretty clothes!"
Saying this he put out his hand and pulled her out.
Seeing that it was Erh-niu, however, he said: "Good!
This time I've caught an underground member of the
Eighth Route Army here! Well, never mind whether
you're Eighth Route or Seventh Route, since you're a
woman in Chiao-chiao's absence you can take her
place! My cousin Chun-hsi thinks you're good-looking:
it's a pity you're rather old! Wash your face and
change your clothes, and we'll see how you look!"
Saying this he tossed Erh-niu the package he had
brought with him.

Just at this moment a shot sounded in the distance
outside, followed by the rattle of machine guns. When
Hsiao-hsi heard the machine guns he hurried to the
door to listen. At first there was only one, but soon
others joined in, intermingling with the explosion of
hand grenades, and Hsiao-hsi's courage failing him,
he hurried off. Taking advantage of his departure
Erh-niu immediately ran into the courtyard to hide in
the long grass.

After a time, when Hsiao-hsi did not come back
but the sound of machine guns and hand grenades
could still be heard, Erh-niu stood up slowly in the
long grass to look far away into the mountains. She
could see flash after flash from the enemy's gun
emplacement, until at last the machine guns and hand
grenades fell silent and the gun emplacement burst
into flames. She ran quietly in to call her mother out
to have a look, and they guessed it must be the Eighth
Route Army back again. After watching the blaze for
a time they went back inside and quietly shut the door

to talk it over with Old Chen, none of them daring to go to sleep for fear that some new trouble might arise.

When it was nearly light Erh-niu's mother said to her: "It's time for you to get quietly away! Don't wait for the daylight when that creature Hsiao-hsi may get after you again!" Erh-niu was afraid of that too, so taking a few cold leaves from the pan for food on the road she stealthily opened the door, slipped out and ran away. When she left the village it was still not light, but she heard people hurrying after her, and was so frightened that she hid again in the tall grass at the side of the road. She heard them pass by talking, and was able to recognize clearly the voices of Li, Hsiao-hsi and Little Mao.

"How many?" asked Little Mao.

"The old Eighth Route Army," said Hsiao-hsi. "Crowds of them, they've filled several villages!"

"Why don't we fight them?" asked Li.

"There are not more than two hundred Japanese troops in the city," said Hsiao-hsi, "and the garrison troops are no use...." By now they were some way off, and she could not hear any more distinctly.

Erh-niu was pleased to know that their guess the previous evening had been correct. She would have given anything to catch those three and hand them over to the Eighth Route Army, but since she was all alone she had to let them go. After they had gone she did not make for Mountain-Back but returned to the village to spread the news. Everybody had seen the gun emplacement go up in flames, and when Erh-niu told what had happened some villagers went to the houses of Little Mao and Li to have a look, and sure enough neither of them was at home, proving that it was true. By this time all the young people had become active again: some went to the gun emplacement to spy out the land, some to the adjoining villages to find the Eighth Route Army. Before breakfast they had a clear picture of the situation—the gun emplacement had been razed to the ground, some of the Japanese inside were dead and some had fled, and the Eighth Route Army had occupied all the villages by the highway. Everybody in the village heaved a sigh of relief. Gates which had been kept barred were opened, young women and children who had not come out into the daylight for a long time came out now into the street, and soon all the grass growing wild in the streets was trodden down.

After Erh-niu had eaten the leaves she decided to go to Mountain-Back to fetch her son. There were more people on the road now, and when they met they exchanged news of how the enemy had been routed. Officers sent out by the Eighth Route Army were coming and going in twos and threes. When Erh-niu had gone half way she met Pai-kou, Chiao-chiao and Little Fatty coming back with Old Wang, for they had already heard the news, and she turned back with them. Pai-kou walked so fast, he left the three others behind. When he met people he knew on the road they all asked how his leg had healed so suddenly, and Pai-kou said: "Now the Eighth Route are here, of course it's better."

By the time Erh-niu and the others reached home Pai-kou came to meet them with a smile: "Here are two Eighth Route we know! Come and see who they are!" Saying this he hurried behind the watch house.

They could hear people talking away at the door. Little Fatty was the first to round the corner, and he immediately shouted: "Mother! Father and Uncle Leng-yuan are back!" When Erh-niu and Wang heard this they both hurried round the corner too. When the others saw them they all burst out laughing and said: "Erh-niu is back too! Mr. Wang is back too!" The youngsters shouted and jumped about like balls pumped full of air which will bounce if you so much as touch them, and all the old folks said to each other: "Like this, even if we only have leaves to eat we feel happier."

Everybody made way as Erh-niu, Little Fatty, Old Wang and Pai-kou pushed through the crowd to where Leng-yuan and Tieh-so were. These two clasped Old Wang's hand, clapped Pai-kou on the shoulder, tousled Little Fatty's head, and, not knowing how to express themselves to Erh-niu, just laughed and said, "So you're back too!"

"Did you and Tieh-so arrange to come back together today?" added Leng-yuan. This set the whole crowd roaring with laughter.

Old Wang and Pai-kou first asked about the other dozen or so men who had left with them, and why they had not come back. Some of their relatives came up to make enquiries.

"The unit we joined hasn't come," said Tieh-so. "They are all very well there, quite a few of them have been given special jobs. Presently I shall go to each of their families in turn to tell them details about them. We two were chosen by our chiefs to come back and work locally—our chiefs said we understood the situation here, so it would be easier for us. So we have been appointed to work in this district."

"That's good," said Old Wang. "Then we can live decently for a day or two."

A few youngsters asked them to make a speech, and Tieh-so said: "All right! You go and fetch people."

"Who is there to fetch?" asked Old Yang. "These are all the people left in the village!" They looked and saw only about a hundred people all told—not even half as many as before.

"Is this all of you?" asked Leng-yuan.

"Yes," said Old Yang. "Some left with you, some were killed by the Kuomintang army and Yen Hsi-shan's troops, some were arrested by the Kuomintang, some were killed or carried off by the Japanese. Then a great many fled, a great many were forced to commit suicide. Think for yourselves, how many could there be left?"

Tieh-so sighed and said, "Well, some is better than none! Let's talk then. In December the year before last, the Kuomintang government ordered the Eighth Route Army to retreat from Chungtiao Mountain and from southeast Shensi, and they sent Kuomintang troops to take over those places. They killed a good many of the people who had resisted the Japanese, and protected a good many traitors, beside causing the death of many of the common people. But later they couldn't protect themselves, and were defeated by the Japanese, leaving those places again for the Japanese to trample underfoot. Now the Eighth Route Army has come back again. And the difference between our coming this time and last time is this—we won't be leaving! We're going to grow roots here! We're going to make this place a centre of anti-Japanese resistance. When we two left we joined the troops, but now we have been transferred here by our superiors to do local work, and allotted to our own district. I'm to be district head and Leng-yuan is to organize a peasants' association. The most important work at present is to re-establish political control, organize the people, and solve the most pressing practical problems. Of course these things can't be done just by talking. Let's first bring up a few practical problems!"

A youngster stood up and said: "Let me first ask something. You tell us: suppose that Kuomintang government or whatever it is issues another order, will the Eighth Route Army leave again or not?"

"Even if they issue a thousand orders, we won't go," said Tieh-so. "We can't hand over our own people again for them to kill!"

"In that case we dare raise problems," said the youngster. "Don't Li and those traitors deserve to be punished? We don't need to wait any longer for Yen Hsi-shan's official order, do we?"

A number of people shouted: "Right! This is the most important question." All gave their attention to this problem.

Some said: "They've already run away, so how can we try them?"

Others said: "The monks can't run away with the monastery."

And some older men said: "Don't be too hasty; we still don't know what will happen later."

But others who understood refuted them, saying, "Don't be afraid of them! What use is it to be afraid? Formerly everyone was afraid of them, but that didn't stop them killing people, did it?"

"This is one question," said Tieh-so. "What other questions are there?" Although some villagers raised problems in connection with famine, farm animals and bandits, they did so half-heartedly. The question of punishing traitors had crowded everything else out of their minds. Seeing how matters stood, Tieh-so and Leng-yuan decided to start with this, for it was one means of mobilizing the masses. So they announced: "Since you all agree that the important thing is to punish the traitors, tomorrow we will make a start. Today it is already late, you had better go home."

After the announcement that the meeting was adjourned Tieh-so turned to Leng-yuan and said: "You ought to go home too and have a look!" And to Erh-niu, "Let's go back and have a look!"

Half-laughing and half-crying, Erh-niu replied, "Where are we to go?"

"That's right," said Old Wang, "Tieh-so hasn't even a house! But now there are so many empty houses in the village, in some courtyards there is not a single person. Just borrow any house you like to live in!"

"I think we should pack Chun-hsi's wife off to her old house," said one youngster, "then Uncle Tieh-so can go back to live in his own."

"That'll have to wait until after their trial," said Tieh-so. And to Erh-niu: "I think tonight we'd better just stay in Dragon King Temple! There's plenty of room there, and can't be anyone staying there." Others agreed that was a good place, since there was only Old Sung there. When the question of meals was raised, Wang said, "Come to my place to eat. My children are only eating leaves, but being an old man I was left some rice."

Leng-yuan and Tieh-so pointed to their ration bags, and said: "We've brought rice."

"You're very well off then," said the others. "We're all eating leaves off trees!"

"I haven't even any leaves," said Erh-niu. After chatting for a time they went home.

That night many people came to the temple to see Tieh-so, saying: "In the houses of Li and his nephews, and in Little Mao's house, they are busily burying things. If their property is to be confiscated, it ought to be done at once; because if we delay they will have hidden everything."

"So long as they don't go out," said Tieh-so, "even if they bury things aren't they still confiscated?"

"That's right," they agreed. "Then we must put in a little time watching them to see that they don't take things out."

"In that case you organize yourselves," said Leng-yuan. They immediately organized about two dozen people to take turns as guards, and posted two sentries at the door of each household.

That evening Erh-niu was so busy telling Tieh-so all that had happened to her during the past year, they did not get to sleep till midnight. They had not been asleep long, however, when there was a hammering at the gate, and when they got up they found the guards had arrested Little Mao. Most of the two dozen men organized earlier in the evening had come too, and they were all in favour of tying him up and giving him a beating.

"Tell the truth!" said Tieh-so. "Where did you run away to? What did you come back for so late at night? If you speak you can avoid a beating!"

When Little Mao saw so many people, he realized he would have to speak, so said: "After we left we kept on going till it was dark, but we didn't succeed in making contact with the Japanese army, and we went to the house of a friend of Landlord Li's. Li stayed there, telling Hsiao-hsi to go and find the Japanese army, and telling me to come back and find out what had happened here. I groped about half the night before I got here, and I hadn't even reached home when those two arrested me!"

"Is Li really staying there?" asked Tieh-so.

"Yes!" said Little Mao.

"Make him take us there to find Li," said some, "and if we don't find him we'll hold Little Mao responsible."

"To make him take us is not a good idea," said others. "When people see we have arrested him they'll tip off Li, and he will be frightened away. It would be better to make him describe the place accurately, and send someone who knows the way to find him. Hold Little Mao here, then if we can't find Li we'll settle all our accounts with him!" Everybody approved of this plan.

"In my opinion," said Tieh-so, "we might enlist the help of the troops in a matter like this. Work has not yet started there, and if only a few peasants go they may not be able to fetch him back!"

"That would be even better," they agreed. So the matter was decided. Tieh-so negotiated with the army, and one squad was ordered out. When the villagers heard they were going to arrest Landlord Li they were wildly excited. The next day Old Wang produced fifteen catties of rice so that those going could have a good meal, and as soon as the troops arrived they set out. Before midnight, sure enough, they had brought Li back.

15

AFTER LI WAS BROUGHT BACK PUBLIC FEELING RAN high. The villagers demanded that he be shot, but Tieh-so as district head could not well make a decision. The county magistrate had come with the army too, and was still living with the troops. The county government and the district administration office had not yet been set up, so there was nowhere to send Li and no place to imprison him. Tieh-so discussed it with the others, and they decided that the villagers should guard Li and Little Mao while he went to see the county magistrate. Accordingly he went to the army, found the county magistrate, and explained the villagers' request regarding these two traitors. The county magistrate considered it would be good to try some cases so soon after his arrival, to let the people know that there was once more political authority for anti-Japanese resistance. Accordingly he agreed to go to the village and give the two men a public trial.

The hall in Dragon King Temple was chosen as the court. The county magistrate sat in the centre, there were ten jurors elected by the village, while Pai-kou and Old Wang had been elected by unanimous vote to act as prosecutors. The entire population of the village had gathered in the temple courtyard to listen. When Li saw how things stood he knew he could expect no mercy, and did his best to put a bold face on it.

As the county magistrate called on the prosecutors to state Li's crimes, someone in the crowd called out: "Pai-kou! No need to mention all he did to cheat people in the past. Just take from after the Kuomintang troops came, up to the present. How many people did he kill? How many did he beat? How many did he drive to suicide? How many poor people did he cheat? How many did he force to run away?"

"All right!" said Pai-kou. "Let's first count the people killed." Then he listed names, and others added a few that he had omitted, bringing the total to forty-two.

When the county magistrate asked Li what he had to say, he answered, "Quite right, these people were killed. Some were killed by the Kuomintang troops, some by the Commandos, some by the Japanese, but not a single one by me!"

"You drew up the lists of names," said Old Wang. "You made the proposals, and anyone you said should die was as good as dead. How can you shift the responsibility now?"

"Judging by what you say," shouted a youngster, "if the county government decides to have you shot, does the county magistrate have to shoot you himself?"

"Think he can talk his way out?" said another. "Every single person in the village who can speak is a witness against him."

Li knew pretty well he could not get out of this, so putting a bold face on it he said, "Even if you take my life for killing some of you, I don't lose by the exchange! I killed forty-two of you, I did pretty well! Go on to something else! I killed all those people! Quite correct!" Since he was so ready to admit it, the rest was easy. All the prosecutors' charges he admitted, and presently they had finished.

After hearing Li's case they tried Little Mao. Little Mao had beaten more people than anyone else; and the prosecutors, unable to estimate the number, said to the crowd: "No need to count those who ran away after being beaten. But those of you here now who have been beaten by Little Mao go over to the left, and those who have not been beaten stand at the right!" When this was done only a few children and young women gathered on the right, practically all the others had moved to the left. And when they were counted the number came to sixty-eight, not including the ten jurors and Pai-kou who was prosecutor.

"Including the jurors and myself that makes seventy-nine," said Pai-kou. "Let him see himself if we've counted wrongly or not."

With only a cursory glance Little Mao said, "I know I beat a lot, and it was wrong. There's no need to count one by one! But I haven't been responsible for a single person's death: it was they who made me arrest people! And I never got any part of the things they cheated you of, just sharing a few meals and some opium with them!"

"You shared their feasts, so you are an accessory!" shouted one of the crowd. "Just drinking their dishwater you still put on high and mighty airs: what would you have done if you had shared in the loot?"

After the cases were heard the whole village demanded that they be shot at once, but the county magistrate was against this. He had been a political worker in the liberated areas, where criminals were spared if there was any hope of their reform. Acting on this principle, he announced: "Judging by their crimes, they deserve to be shot...."

"If they deserve it, then shoot them! There's nothing to be said for them!" shouted the crowd.

"But if they can repent...."

At that there was wild shouting in the crowd: "Don't start that again! They've already repented time and again!"

"If they're not shot, we might as well be dead!"

"Shoot them now!"

"Shoot them at once!"

"Why be so impatient?" asked the county magistrate. "There isn't even a gun here!"

"Just use that revolver you have in your belt!" called someone.

When the county magistrate said he had no bullets, someone else urged: "Just say whether they are to die or not. If they are to die, we can kill them without a gun!"

"They deserved to die long ago..." began the county magistrate.

But without waiting for him to finish, the villagers shouted: "If they deserve to die, hand them over! We'll beat them to death!"

'Throw them down!" they clamoured.

And surging forward they dragged Li out into the courtyard. Seeing this the county magistrate and men in the hall left their seats and went to the front of the hall to watch. Li had been thrown down and villagers had crowded round so closely that they could not see clearly what was happening.

"Take that leg," they heard someone shout.

"Put your foot on his chest!" cried another.

"This won't do!" exclaimed the county magistrate, Leng-yuan and Tieh-so. They pushed their way into the courtyard to stop them, only to find that one of Li's arms had been torn off together with the sleeve of his gown, and the peasants were twisting his face back. His legs had not yet been torn off, but his trousers were already in shreds.

"What do you think you are doing?" shouted the county magistrate. "This is really no good!"

"Whether it's good or not," someone retorted, "at least this is the end of him!"

"Ah," said Leng-yuan, "we ought to listen to the county magistrate."

"We are listening to him!" cried another. "The county magistrate said they deserved to die long ago!"

"That's enough!" said the county magistrate. "There's nothing to be sorry about when such people die, but this way is no good! Making the court swim with blood!"

"Do you call this swimming with blood?" asked Pai-kou. "That day they were killing us, blood from the temple was running out along the gutters!"

The county magistrate went back into the hall, but before he had sat down someone asked, "How about Little Mao?" Little Mao had vanished. Even the county magistrate did not know where he had gone. A search was started in the temple, and Little Mao, realizing he was bound to be discovered, rushed out and threw his arms round the county magistrate's legs and would not let go.

"Magistrate! Magistrate!" he begged. "Won't you let me hang myself?"

Some youngsters said that would not do, and one joker deliberately brought Li's arm to thrust in Little Mao's face, saying: "What do you think this is?"

Little Mao took one look then started trembling convulsively, and kowtowed again and again, saying: "County Magistrate! I—I—I'll hang myself! I'll jump off the cliff!"

Leng-yuan felt rather sorry for Little Mao, and said to him: "What's the use of only pleading with the county magistrate? Haven't you seen the faces of the crowd?"

Hearing this Little Mao let go the county magistrate's legs and turned to kowtow to the crowd, saying: "All you good people! Don't kill me! I'll die! I'll die!"

Seeing this, no one felt like beating him any more, and simply said: "It's time you knew you deserve to die!"

"All go back to your places!" said the county magistrate. And to the jurors: "Let us sit down properly again!"

When order had been restored in the temple, he continued: "Don't take the law into your own hands again! These two men both deserved punishment by death: only if you had allowed them to repent would they have been allowed to live. If you insist on their execution I have to carry out your wishes. But on no account take the law into your own hands. According to the law today, the greatest crime is only punishable by shooting. To tear people to death like that simply won't do."

"County Magistrate!" said Old Wang. "That day when they killed people in the temple they were much more brutal than this—they gouged out eyes, cut off hands, flayed off skins.... I was nearly killed like that!"

"That was their way," said the county magistrate. "But we're not going to copy them, are we? There's still Little Mao. According to him, although he was very cruel, still he didn't kill anyone. Will you give him a chance to repent or not?"

Everybody shouted, "No!"

Then Pai-kou stood up and called out: "Let me make a proposal: I think we should spare him! He won't be able to start any revolt! As long as he will guarantee to make good some of our losses, and apologize properly to everybody, I think we might let him repent!"

Without waiting to see if the others approved or not, Little Mao turned to face the crowd and crawled forward, kowtowing and pleading: "If only you will spare my life, I'll do anything you want! If you really can't spare my life, I ask to be allowed to kill myself. The proverb says, 'Death ends all grudges.' I only ask to die in one piece, then I shall be indescribably grateful!" Having said this he started sobbing.

"How about this," said the county magistrate. "Landlord Li is dead. Let me take Little Mao away with me, and when the county government is set up let us try him again. How about it? What do you all think?"

Some of the youngsters still looked dissatisfied, but made no protest.

"Then let the county magistrate take him back!" urged Pai-kou. "If he has the least intention to reform, why should we kill him unnecessarily? But if he doesn't reform sincerely, this is our world now, and we can always kill him later, can't we?" When he put the case like this nobody had anything to say.

The trial continued, and the prosecutors went on to describe the crimes of Hsiao-hsi and Chun-hsi, and asked that warrants be issued for their arrest. They also requested that the hitherto unconfiscated property of the four families, apart from that required for reparations and relief for the starving, should become public property. The county magistrate straightway announced that these requests of the masses should be carried out. After the trial the verdicts were written out and notices posted up, and that was the end of the business.

In the village, with the help of Leng-yuan and Tieh-so, a Traitors' Property Disposition Committee was organized. Little Mao's property was temporarily sealed up, pending his further trial, but the property of Li and his nephews was immediately confiscated. The land they had cheated people of had already been re-appropriated two years earlier, and this committee endorsed the earlier decision, returning each plot to its rightful owner. A price was fixed for all the movable goods which were used as compensation for the losses, great or small, sustained by each family. The largest item was over three hundred piculs of rice and one hundred and twenty piculs of wheat stored in Li's house. This grain was brought out for the relief of the poor in the village, and at once all the villagers stopped eating leaves.

In a few days the county and district governments were established, and bandits everywhere were mopped up. When the traitors in other villages heard how Li had been beaten to death, they were afraid the people would come to settle accounts with them, and hurried to the county government to give themselves up.

In Li Village the people compelled to run away by Li and those carried off by the Kuomintang army and Japanese gradually came back. The grass in the streets was trodden flat again, and the weeds in the fields were pulled out to make room for sowing a late crop. Old Chen recovered from his illness. Erh-niu and Little Fatty moved back into the house Chun-hsi had cheated them out of over ten years earlier. A village government, national salvation leagues and a militia were set up; but so many of the generation of Leng-yuan and Tieh-so were dead that, apart from Erh-niu who was chairman of the Women's National Salvation League and Pai-kou who was captain of the militia, all the other village cadres were youngsters. The remainder of the traitors' confiscated property was used for communal production in the village, a cooperative being started of which Old Wang was asked to be manager. The people's militia helped the regular army several times to fight bandits, and were given some dozen rifles. About an acre of land belonging to Dragon King Temple was given to Old Sung. All in all Li Village, although it could not compare with the old liberated areas, was beginning to resemble them.

This time Little Mao's repentance was much more genuine than before. He asked the village cadres to take him to the homes of the people he had wronged to apologize, and voluntarily confessed to bad deeds of which they had not known. When they spoke of distributing his property, he just asked to be left enough to keep body and soul together.

Only Hsiao-hsi and Chun-hsi did not come back for trial. Chun-hsi had gone back to Yen Hsi-shan and had not returned, while Hsiao-hsi had fled with the Japanese army to Changchih.

16

AFTER ITS LIBERATION THIS TIME LI VILLAGE NEVER again fell into enemy hands. The Japanese were repulsed several times, and the villagers had good militiamen who skillfully prevented material from falling into enemy hands. There had been three years of severe drought, but the village Mutual Aid Corps opened up canals to irrigate the land, so the crops did not fail. There was a plague of locusts, but the peasants organized a Locust Annihilation Squad, cooperating with the district and county to stamp out the pest, and once again their efforts were crowned with success. In fact, each family produced more grain than originally calculated, and many labour heroes appeared. The cooperative saved a great deal of money, and was expanded to include general goods from all parts, until everything for daily use could be bought in the village. A primary school was set up, also a night school and dramatic troupe; and every evening Dragon King Temple and the entrance to the watch house hummed with activity.

When the news of Japan's surrender reached Li Village the villagers nearly went off their heads with joy—no need to describe how much higher than usual the youngsters jumped, while old people like Wang, Old Chen, Old Sung and Old Yang tugged at their beards and said: "Ho, ho! We've lived to see it, we've worn the Japanese out!"

Front gates that had been blocked up before were opened up again, and things that had been buried for safety were dug up. Once more masons were busy repairing gate houses and roofs burnt by the enemy. Each family hung pictures again in the main hall, and brought out tables, chairs, chests of drawers, stools and mirrors.... Young wives put on the clothes dug up from the ground, and went home to see their families.

The village decided to hold a big meeting on the fifteenth of the eighth month by the lunar calendar (the Moon Festival). They made great preparations for this meeting, and their own dramatic troupe was to perform plays. From the fourteenth to the sixteenth the streets would be filled with lanterns and coloured streamers, and there was to be an exhibition of the victory trophies taken by the village during the war. The programme on the fourteenth included a display by the militiamen of target shooting, hand grenade throwing, bayonet practice, sword practice and other skills. The celebration would be held on the fifteenth. On the sixteenth they would hold a memorial service for all the villagers who had died during the war. And every evening there would be plays.

The morning of the fourteenth the victory trophies were displayed: seventeen Japanese rifles, three revolvers, several dozen hand grenades, one sword, eight steel helmets, over a dozen Japanese overcoats, as well as boots, belts, leather cases, fountain pens, telescopes, picture postcards and maps.... There was enough to fill several tables when properly set out.

After breakfast the target shooting started, each competitor being allowed three shots. When the results were estimated, the average was twenty-three rings, while there were two crack shots who had hit the bull's-eye each time—one of them being the captain of the militia, Pai-kou. The next item was hand grenade throwing. This was not bad either, the average being twenty metres. Little Fatty had practised throwing stones ever since he was a small boy watching cattle, and his throw of thirty-two metres won first place. Everyone praised him as a chip of the old block. In the bayonet and sword practice and free display, there were others who distinguished themselves. When the performance was over they received their prizes in the highest spirits, then went home.

In the afternoon the play started, and in the evening lanterns were lit in the streets and the temple, while amid sounding gongs the performance proceeded. All the youngsters said: "This Moon Festival is the best time we've had since we can remember."

"None of you remember," said Old Wang, "when I was twelve—in the twenty-seventh year of Kuang

Hsü (1901)—the village repaired this Dragon King Temple, and on the Moon Festival we had a performance of a temple-opening play. (That was when we put glass eyes on the Dragon King.) The streets were filled with lanterns then too, only it was not as lively as this time because Li's father was in charge, and in the temple no one dared raise his voice above a whisper."

The next day was the fifteenth, the day for the big celebration. In the morning, while the meeting place was being prepared, a messenger was sent to the district to ask Tieh-so and Leng-yuan to come and join them. After breakfast everything was ready, only Tieh-so and Leng-yuan had not arrived; however, presently Leng-yuan turned up alone.

"Tieh-so has gone to the county seat," he said. "He'll only be able to get here by midday. I left him a note telling him to come on as soon as he got back."

"Then we'll start," said the village head.

The meeting started, the first to speak being the village head. After announcing the purpose of the meeting, he said, "I'll first make a brief summary of the achievements of our village since the war. If you want me to describe in detail all the work in the village during the last eight years from beginning to end, I'm afraid there would be too much, four or five days would not be enough to tell it all. So all we need do now is briefly to compare conditions here now with the past, and in this way we shall see what our chief achievements are. To take the political power first: before the war who dared question any decision of the village administration office? All matters, small or large, were decided by Landlord Li. No one came into Dragon King Temple without breaking into a cold sweat! But what about now? Isn't everything decided by the whole community? Doesn't everybody come to Dragon King Temple in the highest spirits?

"To go on to the livelihood of the villagers: there used to be over eighty poverty-stricken families in the village who didn't have enough to eat, but now there is not a single poor family. In the twelfth month small householders had creditors besieging their doors, and had to beg and borrow right and left to get through New Year, whereas now in the twelfth month everybody can peacefully attend the winter classes or rehearse plays in the dramatic troupe. Everybody can celebrate New Year. In the old days there was constant worry about food and clothing, but aren't things much better now? We don't need to brag about it, each of you knows the facts for himself.

"Then to go on to the reform of bad characters: how many opium addicts were there in the village in the old days? How many gamblers? How many vagabonds, good-for-nothings, thieves and rumour-mongers? I'm not boasting, but can you find a single such person in our Li Village now? In the old days pilfering was rife, but now? The hoe and plough needn't be brought home from the fields in the evening, and when we go to bed at night we don't need to close the front gate—there are no bad people, no thieves. You're all used to this now, and take it for granted; but if you think carefully, would this have been possible before the war?

"Regarding the progress of the whole village, everybody knows about it, so there's no need to say much. Men and women alike can all write their own names now. Old and young alike can all fire a gun. Nowadays these seem very normal things to you, but they wouldn't have been possible before the war! I'm sure that if we were to let loose a few people like Li and his nephews in our village now, they couldn't live! They couldn't cheat people! They couldn't bully people! They couldn't beat people! Nobody would want to borrow money! Nobody would want to buy opium! Nobody would want to gamble! Nobody would call on them! Nobody would pay any attention to them! So how could they live? To put it in a nutshell, the power is no longer in their hands! The power is in our hands now! It's a pity during the last few years the enemy came each year to make trouble for us, but now the enemy has surrendered, our victory is really complete! During the last eight years we have changed that old Li Village into this new Li Village: this is our main achievement!"

When the village head had finished speaking, the captain of the militia, manager of the cooperative, chairmen of the relief associations and school teacher all gave reports of the achievement in their own fields. Leng-yuan also made a speech, and then the meeting was thrown open to discussion. This discussion period was the most lively, because everybody was drunk with victory and had something to say. No matter whether he could speak or not, each had to get up and shout a few words, so that even after midday they had not finished speaking.

Then Tieh-so arrived, and was invited up to the platform to speak. His first words were: "My duty in coming is to tell you all some bad news!"

The whole audience was surprised, each thinking to himself: "After victory what bad news can there be?"

"Japan has already surrendered," went on Tieh-so, "so how can there be bad news?"

"Go on and tell us," people said softly.

"Japan has announced her surrender," continued Tieh-so, "but the Kuomintang government has issued an order forbidding the Japanese to hand over their weapons to us, and ordered the Kuomintang troops to cross the Yellow River to fight the Eighth Route Army. Yen Hsi-shan has joined forces with the Japanese in Shansi, and has returned to Taiyuan, re-cruiting an army from the puppet troops of Hsiao-hsi and his like, telling them to change their insignia and go back to their old stations to mop up the Eighth Route Army. The second time the Eighth Route Army came, didn't they tell everybody they would never leave again? But now those Kuomintang troops are coming, Yen Hsi-shan's troops are coming, and they won't let the Japanese hand over their weapons. You see...."

The villagers started shouting wildly.

"They seem to be very sure of themselves!"

"Where have they been hiding themselves the last few years?"

"What do the authorities plan to do?" asked one.

"Plan?" said Tieh-so. "The Japanese army's guns will still have to be handed over to us! If any one dares come against us, we have only one thing to say! 'Fight it out!' "

Pai-kou leapt onto the platform and said to Tieh-so: "No need to say any more! If they want to come and take this place, I guarantee all our young people will fight to the finish!"

"Right!" shouted the villagers. "It's them or us!"

Pai-kou had already crowded Tieh-so to one side, and standing in the middle of the platform he declared: "Let them come! The last few years we have put by a little grain, just let them come to steal it again! They didn't finish killing everybody here, let them come back to kill the rest! Why should they come back? Is it to avenge Landlord Li? Is it for Chun-hsi to cheat people again? Is it for Hsiao-hsi to play the fool in our homes again? When they are back Third Master can start tying people up, locking people up, beating people up again. Sixth Master can lend out his eighty for a hundred again. Of course they want to come back! But if they come back to make Dragon King Temple flow with blood, will we stretch out our necks again for them to cut our throats? They must be blind! They think we are still the same as a few years ago, only able to stretch out our necks for their swords. We're not the same! Frankly, we can't be treated like dirt any more! After several years of fighting, after attacking cities and towns with the Eighth Route Army, we can all fire a gun! We've some Japanese rifles! We've some Japanese hand grenades! We'll run off again with the Eighth Route Army! We'll get a few more Japanese guns! We'll have a few more encounters with those Kuomintang troops who are coming to attack us! We'll go to invite Hsiao-hsi back again! We'll see how many lives those bastards have!"

Someone in the audience shouted: "First make a list of names of those who want to go!"

"No need to make a list of names!" cried one youngster. "Better line up and let the captain of the militia take his pick—picking out those that are no use, and letting all the rest of us go!"

"Better make a record," said Pai-kou. "If you all agree to register at once, then I'll start making the list!"

They divided into three groups in the court, on the platform and in the hall to register names. When they had finished and pooled their results, there were fifty-three names. Pai-kou saw that some who had registered were over forty, some only fifteen and sixteen. There were women too—the names of Erh-niu and Chiao-chiao were both there.

"Such a group would be rather unmanageable," said Tieh-so. "Better cut it down."

A selection was made, rejecting the old, the young and the women, leaving thirty-seven, including practically all the village cadres. When Tieh-so announced this result Erh-niu, Chiao-chiao and several other women complained, saying they wanted to go to Luan to catch Hsiao-hsi. When Tieh-so told them there was no place for them, they said they could go as nurses. They raised objections for some time, but finally the rest persuaded them to stay at home to head productive work and look after the families of those who were going to fight.

Since all the village cadres were going to fight, substitutes were elected then and there—Erh-niu became acting village head, her place as chairman of the Women's National Salvation League being taken by Chiao-chiao.

"So many people are going to fight," said Old Wang, "there should be someone responsible for seeing that their families are cared for. In addition to looking after the cooperative I can do that too."

That evening nobody wanted to see the play: the volunteers were busy preparing their things, while those staying behind helped them.

The next day the memorial service for those who had been killed was held according to the original plan, but it was followed by another meeting to bid farewell to the volunteers.

The hall in the temple was taken as the hall of sacrifice, and here they set up three memorial tablets. The villagers would never forget Little Chang, so although this meeting was to commemorate the dead of their own village, there was a tablet for Comrade Little Chang in the middle. The tablet on the left was for three militiamen who had lost their lives in resisting the enemy. The one on the right was for the hundred-odd villagers who had been killed or driven to suicide by the reactionaries. A table was placed in front, bearing all manner of sacrificial gifts, and on each side scrolls were hung.

During the memorial service there was funeral music while Chiao-chiao and two other women brought up wreaths of flowers. Then the families of the deceased offered sacrifice, followed by the cadres of the district, the village cadres and villagers. And finally those about to leave for the front offered sacrifice.

The farewell meeting for the volunteers was held beneath the platform, each, as he finished sacrificing, moving back for the meeting. In this meeting, naturally, there were many more speeches, the gist of most of them being: "Li Village as it is today has been bought at the cost of blood, we can't let it be trampled underfoot again.... We are not only avenging the dead, we must also safeguard the living."

After the speeches were over the volunteers took up the guns, ammunition and hand grenades from their war trophies, bowed in farewell to the memorial tablets in the hall, and left Dragon King Temple.

A crowd of villagers beating gongs and drums escorted the small group for a mile. As they parted, each had a farewell message for his own family and friends. Old Wang said to his sons and nephews: "Those scoundrels have got to be driven off, don't let them come here to squeeze me again!"

"Little Fatty!" said Erh-niu. "Remember you're a chip of the old block! Don't go disgracing your father! When you see those rascals, throw plenty of hand grenades at them!"

"If you see Hsiao-hsi," said Chiao-chiao to Pai-kou, "be sure to give him a few bayonet thrusts for me!"

"I won't forget," said Pai-kou. "I've still the scars on my legs to remember him by."